The

Travis

Club

Mark Louis R/
= Hawkeye

The

Travis Club

A Novel

Mark Louis Rybczyk

TH Productions Paperback

Texas

THE TRAVIS CLUB

By

Mark Louis Rybczyk

* * * * *

PUBLISHED BY:

Mark Louis Rybczyk

The Travis Club

Copyright 2013 by Mark Louis Rybczyk

*****

PART I

Chapter 1

Noel Black sharpened a pencil and placed it neatly back in the top drawer of his glass-topped desk, right next to the other sharpened pencils. He glanced at the clock then straightened a few paper clips and a calculator on the stark, polished surface.

11:08 p.m.

He knew he'd be leaving soon. So important to stay on schedule. Especially on a night like tonight, when a life would come to an end.

Among the abstract paintings of his office was one unframed black and white print. A picture of her. Not a picture of sentiment, but simply of record. A photo that would soon belong in a file.

Black fingered the yellowed photograph and could not help but think of childhood visits to his mother's father, his *abuelo*. He remembered spending the hot San Antonio summers at a rickety west-side duplex much different than his parents' ranch house in Dallas. Abuelo's home was filled with people, music, food and love.

As a child, Black would spend summer afternoons within earshot of the front window, waiting for the rumble of his grandfather's old diesel engine. Then the home would fill with other workers, workers who were grateful to the old lady. All immigrants, they had left Mexico hoping for a better life. The old lady offered them higher wages than the pecan shellers received. With the promise of steady income came the chance to move into a house with plumbing, to send money home, and to send for other relatives. His grandfather loved the old lady and he did too.

More recently, Noel Black's feelings about her had changed. She was a relic, an icon of a past era. Now in her final years of the 20th century, the old lady had outlived her usefulness and had no place in the modern San Antonio that he envisioned. She was in his way. She needed to be eliminated.

Of course, this kind of work had to be contracted out. He usually relied on a local contact who understood the procedures. Anytime a life was extinguished, it must be done with precision in Noel Black's world.

11:22 p.m.

38 minutes to show time. His instructions were explicit: action not to be taken until midnight. Not a second sooner. Not a moment later.

He locked the glass door behind him and walked briskly to his polished black BMW. He knew that he should stay and wait for a call. But tonight, waiting was too difficult.

11:37 p.m.

He eased the perfectly waxed sedan through the streets of downtown and into the fringes of the west side. "This land is way too valuable," he mumbled aloud. He slowed down and parked across the street, hoping to be inconspicuous, even though he knew that a European sedan was about as common in this South Texas *barrio* as a snowball.

"Just a quick look," he told himself.

He caught the eye of a shadowy figure in a black hooded sweatshirt. It was one of the locals he had hired to complete the job. Black flashed back the *mal ojo*, the evil eye. He knew he shouldn't have come. But deep inside he needed to see her one last time, not to pay his respects, but to make sure the job was done right.

11:46 p.m.

He started up his engine and allowed his eyes one final glance at her. It was one time too many. Immediately, he noticed something amiss. A glint behind a window pane that made him realize someone must have been tipped off.

He felt a rock in his stomach. He knew there would be trouble.

Chapter 2

At 11:46 p.m. Taylor Nichols pulled his old pickup into the driveway. A flurry of cats scattered from the carport as he alit and walked around to open the truck's passenger side door. From the downstairs apartment of the ancient house an old woman looked out at her neighbor and smiled in disbelief. "A girl," she thought. "He's finally with a girl!"

"I have never seen so many gray cats in all my life," Taylor's date said, laughing. "They're all gray."

"Most of them belong to my downstairs neighbor, Mrs. Floraman," Taylor replied. "She refuses to get her cats fixed, so the neighborhood is flooded with gray cats. Every fool on this street has adopted one." The couple walked up the back steps to the upstairs apartment, where another cat, also gray, meowed as they unlocked the door.

"Is he yours?" she asked.

"That's Mister Tibbs," said Taylor.

"Would you like a cat?" came a wobbly voice behind them. The old woman had quietly followed the pair up the stairs. "Aren't you going to introduce me to your lovely date, Taylor?"

"Logan Pierce, this is my neighbor, landlord and surrogate mother of the entire Alta Vista Neighborhood, Edna Floraman," Taylor said.

"Don't roll your eyes, Taylor," the old lady scolded. "So pleased to meet you, dear; and how did you meet my Taylor?"

"I work at Alamo National Bank, and I met Taylor when he came in for a car loan."

"Car loan!" scoffed Edna. "He can barely pay his rent. I don't know how he can afford a new car. The world's worst selling author, that's who you're dealing with."

"Well, actually I had to turn him down," Logan said sympathetically, "but I felt so sorry for him I asked him out to dinner."

"Thank you, Mrs. Floraman. Your intrusion has made me realize that I'm on a sympathy date."

"A least you got a date," the old woman said while being shown the door. "Most handsome single man in the city and he spends all his time at the library. All the gays in this neighborhood and the one straight man won't even bring a girl home. I'm tired of defending you to the old bats on Lynwood Street."

"Good night, Mrs. Floraman," Taylor said as the screen door clattered shut. Just before she got out of earshot, she started to hum "Some Enchanted Evening," much to the amusement of Taylor.

"She's right, you know," said the striking brunette, finally finding herself alone with the young Taylor. "You are the most handsome single man in the city."

"Oh, really? Two minutes ago I was your sympathy date."

"Taylor, all the women swoon when you come into the bank. I've waited for months to meet you. I was breathless when you walked to my desk." She moved slowly toward him and put her arms around him.

"I noticed you found enough breath to reject my loan application."

"Forgive me, but you barely make $12,000 a year. How are you going to pay for a new truck?" she purred, moving closer.

"I'll have money when my next book is finished. I still can't figure out why you decided to go out with me."

"Excuse me, I believe it was I who asked you out," she whispered in his ear.

"Better yet, why did you ask out a struggling writer who has no money and drives a beat-up old truck without air conditioning?"

"First of all, you are not a struggling writer. If I recall from your application, you have a 10-book deal."

"Yes, but only the first two books made any real money," he answered.

"Second, if I knew your truck hadn't any air conditioning I would have insisted we take my car."

"Sorry about the truck; I want to buy a new one but the evil woman at the bank turned down my loan," he joked, as she slowly pulled him closer. It had been a long time since he had been on a date. He could feel her breath drawing closer to his lips when the tinny ring of his rotary phone rattled the room. "Damn," he whispered.

"Let it ring," she said, as she pulled him back to her arms.

"I've really got to answer it. I'm expecting a call."

"It's nearly midnight on a Friday; who calls at this hour?" she asked over another ring.

Her hands moved slowly down his back as her lips eased toward his. He wanted so desperately to yank the cord from the wall. It seemed like years since he had felt so sure of himself. Still, he willed his hand toward the receiver and lifted it to his ear.

"Hello?"

Recognizing the voice on the phone, he pushed her away and rose. "Yes, tonight…Black doesn't miss a trick…I'm on my way."

Taylor hung up and rushed for the door. "Where are you going? What about the rest of our date?"

"I've got to go," he spurted, darting for the door while barely noticing her disappointment.

"What about me?" she said, pouting.

He paused and looked back. "You can come, but it might not be pretty."

Chapter 3

The Finck Cigar and the Travis Club

"In the late 19th century, cigar making was a popular Texas industry, especially among the newly arrived German immigrants. Freidrich Ernest, the father of German Immigration in Texas, was himself a cigar maker. Only one cigar manufacturer remains today: the Finck Cigar Company of San Antonio. When H.W. Finck, a second generation German-American, set up shop in San Antonio, the city was already home to 18 other manufacturers. At the time, most American cities had a handful of cigar makers, the majority being one-man operations.

The Fincks lived upstairs from their business and later opened a small but ornate factory that employed many newly-arrived Mexicans from the city's west side. The Fincks' ability to adapt to a changing industry is one reason the company was able to survive.

In 1910 Finck made a special cigar for members of the Travis Club. The Travis Club was an elite social club for prominent San Antonians with a multi-storied building downtown for its clubhouse. The cigar was for members of the Travis Club only. During World War I, the club also opened its doors to servicemen, who made it a popular hangout. So popular, in fact, that there was little room left for the members. After the war, the members failed to return and the club folded. However, the Travis Club cigar lived on. The Finck Company was flooded with orders from servicemen who had sampled the smoke during their stay in the city. Thus began the Travis Club brand.

Today the company is still going strong, as is the Travis Club brand cigar, which can now be purchased by the general public. The Fincks, now in their fourth generation of cigar making, continue to adapt to a changing world, and opened their most recent factory in 1970. The original factory still exists on the outskirts of downtown and is being considered for redevelopment."

From the book *Gone But Not Forgotten, A Look at Vanished San Antonio Landmarks and Institutions*, by Taylor Nichols

* * *

"Where are we going?" asked Logan.

"I'll explain on the way," Taylor shouted as he ran into the garage. "Just get in the truck." The old Ford sputtered for a moment or two before its engine finally turned. Taylor gunned her out of the driveway and raced down San Pedro Avenue toward downtown.

"Before I die in this un-air-conditioned deathtrap, do you mind telling me where we are going?"

"We're having a meeting of the Travis Club."

"Oh, I see, the Travis Club. I hope I'm dressed appropriately," she said sarcastically. "What the hell is the Travis Club?"

"Watch your language. It's very poor manners to swear, especially on the first date." The truck screamed through a red light and turned a corner toward the west side of downtown. "Have you ever heard of the Finck Cigar building?"

"Isn't it that old building that has been in the paper, the one that Noel Black is trying to redevelop?"

"Trying to redevelop, Noel Black? Ha! That's a laugher. That robber baron would tear down the Alamo to build a parking lot if he could make an extra dime!" retorted Taylor.

"Would you please make some sense before my life ends in this 1964 Ford Deathtrap?" she begged.

"This is a 1965 Ford F-100 Deathtrap that I only own because I couldn't get a loan from your bank," he said pointedly.

"Whatever. Just please make some sense of what's happening."

"In a nutshell, Noel Black, the famed Dallas developer, owns the historic Finck Cigar Building, sometimes called the Grand Old Lady of the West Side. Through the press he has made it seem like he plans to redevelop the building. But all along he has planned to tear the place down."

"That's crazy! Why would he do that?"

"Because he could make a lot more money building a steel and glass high-rise on the property instead of owning a quaint old cigar factory."

"I'm still confused. Isn't that building protected by the city's Historic Preservation Code?"

"It was," he explained, "but when an abandoned building is designated a historic property, that designation only lasts 90 days. If no one renews it, the owner is free to tear it down. That designation expires at midnight tonight. We won't be able to renew the protective act until 8:30 in the morning. That gives Black about eight hours to tear down the building."

"I still don't get it," she said. "I don't know of any plans to build on that lot. If there was some sort of financing for a big project, every banker in town would know about it."

"That's the worst part; he doesn't have any plans. At least no formal plans. But nonetheless, he may never have another opportunity to tear down the building. He'll just pave over the grounds and make another parking lot, then wait until the furor dies down before he tries to get money. Plus, if there is no building, then his property taxes will be a lot less."

"How do you know all this? How can you be sure he's going to tear down the building tonight?"

"The rest of us have camped out inside the building. We suspected that Black would try something. If we don't hurry, the whole Finck building could be gone in the blink of an eye." He raced along the edge of downtown, barely missing a group of tourists outside Market Square. The well-lit streets quickly changed into dark, lonely corridors surrounded by warehouses and unused buildings.

"You keep saying 'us' and 'we.' Who's 'we?'" she asked.

"The Travis Club."

* * *

By the time the old Ford reached the ancient cigar factory, mayhem had broken out. The red and blue lights of half a dozen police cruisers reflected off the decaying building. "By the way, Logan, have you ever spent a night in jail?"

"Jail?"

"Some of my friends might get arrested tonight."

"Arrested? Arrested for what?"

"Black is probably going to have us arrested for trespassing."

"Can he do that?"

"Sure, we're trespassing."

The pair raced across the street and through a maze of television satellite trucks. A black sedan had pulled up next to the old factory.

"We've got quite a party; police, reporters, and even Black thought to make an appearance," remarked Taylor. Inside the factory the scene was no less chaotic. Most of the activity centered on the first floor restroom, where five people had chained themselves to a toilet. By then, police officers had given up trying to keep straight faces as one readied a pair of bolt cutters.

"Please don't cut the chain," shouted Joe Reyes, the ringleader. "There's no lock; it's just tied in a knot behind the can."

"There's no lock? This is incredible! What a bunch of imbeciles. I can't believe the San Antonio Police Department cannot provide me with protection! I want all these people arrested!" shouted Noel Black.

"For what? Tying themselves to a toilet with a chain?" shouted back the officer.

"First of all, I believe your records will show a temporary restraining order against the gentlemen of the Travis Club. They've been ordered to stay at least 500 yards from any of my property.

Joe Reyes cleared his throat. "Mr. Black, I believe the key word in the term 'temporary restraining order' is *temporary*. If you check, you'll see that it expired two weeks ago."

"Officer, I believe trespassing is still against the law. I want these cretins unchained from my toilet immediately.

"Have you seen that toilet? If you want them untied from there, you do it yourself," said the officer, now openly laughing. Everybody, in fact, was laughing, including the television crew filming the event, which further incensed Black.

"Taylor Nichols! There he is! He's the one behind all of this! I want him arrested too!" bellowed the man.

"For what? Conspiracy to commit a sit in at a men's room?" roared the officer. He raised his hand to signify that the fun was over. "Okay, listen up. If you're chained to a toilet, then untie yourself and get in the police van. If you own a historic building that has people chained to the men's room commode, then come downtown with an officer. If you are a TV newsman, then finish up and go home. If you happen to be a certain writer and radio talk show host who probably will end up bailing out the rest of his merry crew, meet us downtown where we can sort all this out. Now we all know the procedure, so let's clear out and clean up like we've done a dozen times before."

The five people disentangled themselves and were led to the police van. As they passed Taylor, the young writer grabbed the chain gang's ringleader. "You tied the chain in a *knot*?"

"Do you know how much a good lock and chain cost? I've bought eleven locks and chains and eleven have been cut in half by the police. Do any of the other guys ever offer to buy the chains? No, it's always me who has to spring for the hardware."

"Look at this. Quite amusing, isn't it? Five ragtag hooligans chained to a toilet once again manage to halt progress," said the sharply-dressed man. "Taylor Nichols, we meet again in our usual setting."

"Noel Black, my pleasure as always," said Taylor sarcastically.

"Hello, asshole," said Joe.

"Joe, please. Your language is not appropriate when addressing our state's premier developer."

"Well excuse me! Hello, 'Mister' Asshole."

Taylor fought to hold back his own laughter. "Black, I don't understand you. Why did you buy this building when you only intended to tear it down? Why can't you buy some vacant lot and build on that?"

"Mr. Nichols, my motives are not up for discussion. What buildings I decide to buy and what I decide to tear down is none of your concern.

"Wrong! It *is* my concern. This is everybody's city, not just yours. We will decide what pieces of history we want to protect. That right belongs to the public."

"One man's history is another man's burden. You are the one who has accepted the burden, not I. I own this property; I decide what is to be done with it." He spun on his polished wing tips and strode toward the door. "Mr. Nichols, you may have won the battle, but you will not win the war. This building will come down. You cannot stop me."

"I wouldn't count on that."

* * *

"This is Russell Rhodes, Eyewitness News. As has happened many times in recent years, historical activists have chained themselves inside a landmark building that they believed was about to be secretly torn down. Developer Noel Black, who owns the abandoned Finck Cigar Factory, joins us from outside the building, where five protesters have apparently stopped the demolition.

"Mr. Black, can you explain what happened here tonight?"

"Russell, I got a call from the police that some vandals were camped out in the Finck building with gas cans. Their intent I can only guess. I do not know why anyone would want to destroy this historic structure. Luckily I was able to get here in time and catch the arsonists before they completed their evil."

"Mr. Black, isn't it true that you intended to have this building destroyed by 8:30 this morning, when the Historic Review Board will renew a protective order that would make it illegal to destroy the Finck Building?"

"Russell, that is simply not true."

* * *

From a distance, a shadowy character watched the proceedings. Far enough away not to be noticed, he was still able to keep a close eye on the main characters in this strange morality play. He jotted a few notes on a pad and watched as the police cleared the area. After the scene had settled into the night he returned to his car. He stopped at an abandoned pay phone and dropped a coin into the slot.

"Yes, I'm here now," he mumbled into the phone, "and you were right. This Taylor Nichols is the one."

* * *

The sleepy police precinct quickly filled with activity when the transport van unloaded Taylor and the rest of the Travis Club.

A worried Taylor got out of the police van. "Oh, no. I just remembered I was on a date."

"Hey Major, she wouldn't happen to be that beautiful brunette in the corner?" teased Joe.

Logan smiled from the corner with the keys to the old Ford in her hand. "I don't know what happened, who is who, or why I'm at a police station at one in the morning."

"Who's the girl, Major?" teased Joe.

"I'm sorry. Logan Pierce, meet my favorite con, Joe Reyes."

"Excuse me, lovely lady, but I need to get booked."

As Joe and the rest of the club checked in, Taylor sheepishly apologized. "If you forgive me, I'll take you to the most romantic spot in San Antonio."

"How can I resist those beautiful brown eyes? Besides, I have a weakness for outlaws. Can we go?"

"In a few moments. The guys are being booked, then I'll bail them out and we can go."

"What's going to happen to them?"

"If the charges aren't dropped, they will get a suspended sentence or community service. It's not like they are going to send a man to prison for chaining himself to a toilet."

The crew of five lined up and waited for the police sergeant to call their names and post bail.

The first to come through was Joe. If Taylor was the soul of the Travis Club, Joe was the brains. He was the guy who formulated the plan, the guy who could always figure out the best way to throw a monkey wrench into the cog. He was also the only one of the guys to have a decent paying job. Joe graduated from St. Mary's Law School and bypassed the corporate world in favor of hanging his own shingle. His practice was not lucrative, but it provided nicely for him and his wife, Ella.

Though Ella did not make a habit of trekking through abandoned buildings in the middle of the night, she definitely was a kindred spirit. Her generosity had provided many meals for the crew when the dollars were few and their appetites were plenty. She worked while Joe completed law school and always made sure he had the time to finish his studies. When Joe graduated and decided to start his own practice, it was Ella who worked the long hours as receptionist, office manager, secretary, and paralegal. She also lent her support to Joe when the Travis Club started to get a bit more involved. Tonight, though, she had decided to bypass the festivities. Hanging around the police station in the middle of the night was where she drew the line.

Joe's handcuffs were removed as Taylor whipped out a wad of bills to pay his bail. The large amount of money surprised Logan, but only because she had not seen Joe slip him an envelope in the police van. It was always Joe who paid the bail, and, as of yet, no one had ever skipped out. As a matter of fact, the Travis Club was a well-oiled machine when it came to this sort of thing. When a historic building was about to be demolished without the group's approval, their plan went into action. Usually they only needed to stop the bulldozers and demolition crews long enough to find a judge and issue a restraining order until city council could renew the Historic Preservation Ordinance. The easiest way to do this was to chain themselves to the building the night after the ordinance expired. Because of a quirk in the city code, one could not renew a protective order on a historic building until after it expired. Thus, there was usually an 8-hour window for the developer to tear down the building if he chose to. Joe was working the legal ends to close this loophole, but considerable opposition from developers had slowed the effort.

The chaining, though, proved quite effective. Usually, an unscrupulous developer would hire a demolition crew with explicit instructions to tear the building down at 12:01 a.m. Upon arriving with detonation equipment, however, the crew would find a group of people chained to the building. Soon, the police would be called, usually by the Travis Club themselves, and they would be arrested for trespassing. The police would take everybody downtown to sort out the mess and post a patrol car there until the morning to protect the building from further "trespassers." Once, a builder hired a guard to keep the Travis Club away the night of the supposed destruction. This tactic turned out to be futile because the group instead chained themselves to a stop sign and strung out into the street blocking traffic and creating a general nuisance.

Joe Reyes knew that two things needed to be done after the crew was arrested. First, they need to be bailed out. Since he was the only one with any money, this task fell into his lap. Usually one member of the Club would be "on call". Simply put, he would be home by 11:30 p.m. waiting for a call to come down to the arrest site, ride down to the police station, and bail everybody out. In most cases Joe would slip him an envelope with enough money to cover the expense. Joe would recover the bail money when and if the trial ever made it to court. Usually, the sentence was suspended, occasionally community service was prescribed, and the city gained five overqualified graffiti cleaners or dog walkers. Joe's second task took place the next morning when he appeared at municipal court at 8:30 to have the protective order renewed.

Once, Noel Black tried to outwit the Travis Club, tearing down a historic Humble gas station the day before the ordinance expired so he could provide 12 more parking spaces outside a new mall. Black was hoping that the judge would believe that a clerical error was the reason behind the destruction. The judge decided to make Black rebuild the station from the rubble at considerable cost and warned him that a jail term and great embarrassment would follow if this sort of "clerical error" ever occurred again.

The next member to be released was Steve Sommers. Steve had first met Joe when they were both undergrads at San Antonio College and worked at a record store near campus. While Joe graduated and went on to finish law school, Steve continued to change majors and schools at whim. At San Antonio College he studied photography. At Our Lady of the Lake University it was architecture. He changed his major to art after transferring to St. Mary's University. The others joked that he would someday have to rent a U-Haul to collect his transcripts. He was the classic perpetual student. He had over 120 credit hours but had changed his major so many times that he always seemed to be two years away from graduation. It seemed to everybody that Steve's real plan was to marry someone like Ella, who would support him while he wandered his way through school. But few women were interested in a long-term relationship with a man who had no direction.

One of the few places he did seem to be going was Joe's house. He practically lived there, sponging off free meals, sleeping on the couch on Saturday nights, and generally overstaying his welcome.

Steve was the king of thrift. His main source of income was hanging posters for upcoming movies or selling t-shirts at concerts. He was always coming up with ingenious ways to earn money. His most recent, and most infamous, scheme was the taco car. Steve used chicken wire and plaster build a giant taco around his 1972 Volkswagen Beetle. He cut a deal with Big Ern's Crispy Tacos and painted the greasy spoon's name on the side of the tortilla in exchange for $300 and five free meals a month. In any other city, a man driving a giant taco would be an outcast. In San Antonio he became a celebrity. Nonetheless, he was celebrity with friends who would rather walk than be caught dead in the "meal on wheels".

Steve rarely shopped at a retail store, but was a regular customer at the Salvation Army's main thrift shop. His main purchase was white oxford shirts that had been old Catholic school uniforms. The thrift store had hundreds of them that sold for 50 cents apiece. Each week Steve would buy seven freshly laundered used shirts from the store, wear one a day with a pair of jeans, and on Friday re-donate them to the Salvation Army and buy seven more. With the cleaners charging a dollar for a laundered shirt, he figured he saved $3.50 a week or $182 a year.

Eric Bob Kaufman King was the next to post bail. Eric Kaufman was his real name, but he earned the name Bob King at his first radio disc jockey gig. He hated the name Bob King, but he wanted the job so he took the moniker. Later he learned that the radio station had a set of musical jingles pre-made with the name Bob King and that the last three guys who held the job were also given the name Bob King. To the bank and his parents, he was known as Eric Kaufman. But among his friends it quickly became Eric Bob Kaufman King. It was Eric Bob who first convinced Taylor to host a radio talk show. The pair had met in college. Both lived on the same floor of the dormitory. Eric (as he was known then) was one of the few guys from San Antonio who lived in the dorm, and he and Taylor fast became friends.

Often on the weekends they would explore San Antonio's "hidden treasures." One weekend they sought to find the lost pool of the Hot Wells Hotel. The long closed hotel on the south side of town was in a dilapidated state, but the spring-fed pool was said to be in excellent condition. The duo jumped a fence, only to be quickly captured by the old caretaker who lived on a mobile home adjacent to the abandoned hotel. He told them that the pool was a myth and that they would have to leave or he would call the police. Later that night, Taylor and Eric Bob snuck back onto the property to find the old caretaker swimming in a perfectly preserved sulfur pool in the middle of the hotel's ruins.

The final two to be released were the Guenther brothers, Ted and Ed. The pair worked for their father in the world's most disorganized bookstore. Poor Broke Guenther, as he referred to himself, owned a two-story building filled from basement to roof with used books. Every now and then, the Guenther Brothers would find some long-forgotten gem. One day, in an old box marked "yearbooks," they found a photo album that contained pictures of Geronimo taken during his internment at Fort Sam Houston in San Antonio. Taylor was later able to use the photos in one of his books.

An optimist would look at the store in the hopes of organizing the materials and taking inventory of the unknown treasures. A realist would look at the store and surrender.

The Guenther brothers were realists. In fact, they hated the bookstore. They could not wait for the day their father would let them leave and discover what life held for them. But he made them feel guilty for wanting a life of their own and told them it was their obligation to work in the store, because someday it would be theirs. To Ted and Ed, however, the bookstore was their own private purgatory.

As soon as the whole gang was released, Joe broke out a box of Travis Club cigars. After every arrest it had become a tradition to pass out the locally made cigars to the officers as a way of thanking them for their understanding. Throughout the force, the cigars became a prized memento; the officers involved in the arrest would proudly display the cigar in their right pocket, much to the envy of their peers. After the first few arrests, Taylor and the rest became known simply as the Travis Club to the men in blue.

* * *

It was now two in the morning. The club made plans to meet for breakfast in the morning. Tomorrow was Saturday, and it was a tradition to meet at the end of the week to discuss "club business," which usually consisted of Joe complaining how much he has spent on locks and chains. As for Taylor, he had one more promise to keep.

Chapter 4

The streets of downtown were deserted. The faint click of glasses carried down the River Walk as clubs and restaurants cleaned up for the night. Logan and Taylor parked on St. Mary's Street across from the Tower Life Building and crept up to the door of the historic skyscraper.

Taylor peered through the glass, waiting for the opportune moment.

"Why are we sneaking around like this?" queried Logan.

"Shhhhhh," hissed Taylor, choking back a laugh. His eyes fixed on the security guard seated in the vestibule. When he stood and ambled down a corridor, Taylor grabbed his date and dashed through the front door and past the rickety folding table. He pushed the elevator button, and as they fidgeted before the ornate brass doors, footsteps could be heard from around the corner.

"Damn you, Taylor; I sees you, you no fool nobody," shouted the guard. The doors finally slid apart and the couple darted in. "I sees you, I sees you," he said, the hint of a smile in his thick German accent. He arrived just in time to stick his arm in the crack. "Taylor Nichols, you no supposed to come back to my building."

"Ah, come on Karl, this is a big night. I have a date."

"I see that you do. Allow me to introduce myself. Karl Guenther, Tower Life Building Security Officer. You, my lady, are trespassing on private property and I would arrest you myself except I have a feeling that you already have spent time tonight in the police station with this scoundrel." With that he exploded with laughter and let the door slide shut. "Remember, be back by sunrise so Karl Guenther does not face the wrath of his superiors," his voice echoed, fading as they rose. "Ha ha ha ha."

Taylor had pushed the button for the 31st floor. Logan chuckled as the elevator lumbered to the top. "That security guard was quite a character. Do you come here often?"

"Karl. I've known him for years. That's Ted and Ed's uncle."

"You promised you would take me to the most romantic place in San Antonio. I must say that I didn't think we were going to sneak into 'Uncle Karl's' office building," Logan said.

"Just wait. You'll see that beauty can be found in the most unusual places."

The elevator stopped at the summit and the two walked into a paneled foyer. On one side loomed a mahogany door with "Law Offices of Benjamin Goldstein" etched into the glass. A brass door was to their right. Taylor took Logan's hand and led her through it into the building's stairwell. Before floor 31, the stairwell was gray and drab, but marble encased the final two flights of stairs they climbed. A number of doors greeted them on the top floor, including the Men's and Ladies rooms.

Logan hesitated as Taylor tugged her toward the Men's room. "Please don't tell me that we're going to chain ourselves to one of the toilets."

"Trust me," he said softly. The pair walked into a small but clean restroom where Taylor unbolted a lock and pushed up the window. "Follow me." He stepped on the toilet lid, squeezed his shoulders through the window frame and reached a hand back. "Come on. Trust me."

Logan hesitated again, then stepped gingerly onto the toilet, unsure of what she was getting into. Over the course of a few hours, she had bounced through a high-speed race across town in Taylor's rickety truck, seen his friends chained to plumbing fixtures in an abandoned factory, then found herself in the police station as the arrested perps were bailed out. Now she was supposed to climb on top of a toilet and shimmy through a window. The nicest word to describe this date, she decided, would be "interesting." Wriggling out and shaking the dust from her hair, she realized she was on the floor of an open balcony. She gained confidence and rose to peer over the wall, and the view made her draw her breath in. The city of San Antonio in all its nighttime splendor spread before her in a private showing. "Oh my," she whispered. "It's beautiful."

"I told you to trust me."

"What is this place?" she said.

"My own private observation deck."

"Well, aren't you lucky. Really, what is this?"

"This is the Tower Life Building, for years the tallest building in San Antonio, and for that matter, the tallest west of the Mississippi. It was the Empire State Building of San Antonio. This was the observation deck. When the World's Fair came to San Antonio in 1968, the Tower of the Americas was built, which features a higher observation deck, thus putting this grand old lady out of business. For the most part, it sits empty. I feel as if I'm the only person left who still appreciates her."

"You and your friends seem to appreciate a lot of things that others don't."

"Let's just say that we see beauty where others see profits. We see potential where others see decay."

"I look now and all I see is beauty."

"I must be rubbing off on you. Next thing you know, you'll be ready to chain yourself to a toilet."

"I don't think so," she chortled. She stood in silence, taking in the glittering vista. "This is the perfect end to a very strange evening."

"Strange?"

"Come on, Taylor, I haven't had many dates take me to the police station to bail out their friends. But there are still some things I don't get. While you were rescuing your buddies, I was talking to Joe, and he explained what all was taking place. But I don't understand what's going to happen in the morning. I saw three television stations there. By afternoon everybody will know how Black tried to tear down the building. With that kind of negative publicity, won't he back down?"

"Negative publicity?" He laughed. "If he can help it, there won't be any publicity. Tonight, Black will make some discreet calls to station managers and make sure the story won't make it to the air. The only guy who ever gets the story on the air is Russell Rhodes from Channel 5, but every time it's a struggle."

"I don't understand. How can Black get a story killed?"

"It's done all the time. Black's enterprises are far-reaching. He might threaten to pull some advertising dollars on one station; he might know an owner who has some political aspirations and can use a nice contribution from his lobbying group. Journalists like to pretend it doesn't happen, but it does, all the time.

"That's why we have to do what we do. We can't use traditional means to battle developers who have no interest in our hometown other than to turn a quick profit. See the lights out there? Those are the people who pay the taxes, who teach our children, who build our roads, our parks, our schools, who make our city work. This is their home. Shouldn't they have the right to say how their city is shaped and formed? Noel Black doesn't live in San Antonio. He just sees this city as a giant theme park, a place to make a dime. Is it right that he should be allowed to come to our home and tear down our history, our past?"

"Your argument sounds great, but I just saw five guys chain themselves to a building they had entered illegally. Doesn't he have the right to do with his property as he pleases?"

"That's the stupidest thing I've ever heard," he said, with a bitter laugh.

"Why is that so stupid?" she asked defensively.

"Well, because you're right." Taylor sighed and gazed far off into the lights. "But, the point is that he can build his new skyscraper on a dozen sites. Why must he choose a piece of land that a historic building sits on? A building that says who we are and where we came from. And then he lies to us. He tells the public he intends to restore these buildings, then tears them down so he won't have to pay the taxes. Why does he even bother to buy them in the first place? Half the time these guys tear down a building only to leave it a vacant lot for 10 years or longer. Sure, it's his building. He bought it. But if he bought the Mona Lisa would that give him the right to take a razor blade and slash it? In theory it may, but it would still be wrong."

Logan hugged Taylor from behind and kissed his cheek. "I know," she whispered into his ear. "I know what you mean."

"And I know what you mean. It's just that we would like Black to step back and really look at the buildings he wants to tear down. Why can't he understand the potential behind some of these places? Look over there; what do you see?" Taylor pointed to the Rivercenter, the shopping and hotel complex surrounding part of the River Walk.

"I see the Rivercenter."

"Do you know what used to be there before they built it? The Fairmont Hotel."

"What? That's five blocks away."

"Exactly! The Fairmont was a vacant four-story hotel that spent years decaying in an abandoned lot. When the Rivercenter project was approved, nobody knew what to do with the old hotel. Someone suggested picking up the entire structure and moving it to another part of downtown. It took months to prepare for the move. Thousands showed up to see the building inching through the streets of downtown. At one point they had to cross a bridge over the River Walk without knowing if it would hold. The Fairmont is now in the Guinness Book of World Records as the largest structure ever moved. And you know what became of that old, abandoned, decrepit hotel?"

"Yes. It's now one of the most exclusive hotels in the city, if not the state."

"Exactly. See, someone else saw potential where others only saw a roadblock to progress." Taylor pointed to the North Side. "You see that building over there?" Logan shifted her focus to one of the newer skyscrapers that dotted the cityscape. "The Republic Bank Building. Twenty-five stories of shining glass and steel. At the bottom stood the façade of the old Texas Theater. One of the grandest movie theaters ever built."

"I've always wondered what the story was behind that building," Logan said.

"I could almost write a book on that building, it has so many stories. Originally the corner of Houston and St. Mary's streets was the busiest intersection in town.

At its apex sat the Texas Theater, the Majestic and the Empire, with the Aztec just a block away. But, in the late seventies, these grand old ladies started showing their age. Instead of first run movies they had become home to heavy metal concerts, skin flicks, and second run features. But people had a vision that one day, the four theaters could be restored to their past glory, that they could host visiting Broadway shows, concerts, the symphony, the opera, and recitals. Well, the Majestic, the Aztec and finally the Empire all were brought back to life, but the Texas Theater never made it."

"Part of it did."

"Yeah, only the façade. You see, Republic Bank ... "

"Of Dallas," she chimed in.

"Well I wasn't going to point that out, but yes, Republic Bank of Dallas wanted to build a big office complex in San Antonio and they wanted to build it in the same location as the Texas Theater. The preservationists wanted to save the theater, but the developers wanted no part of it. The Conservation

Society even paid an architect to draw up a new set of plans that would have preserved the theater and built the offices atop the old building. But the bank wanted no part of it. The whole thing ended up in court, and the bank won. The conservationists threatened to go back to court, and the parties struck a compromise of some sort. The bank would save the façade of the old building and build around it.

Now it just stares out at the street. Whenever I go by there, I feel like I'm looking at a beautiful woman who has lost her soul. I remember when they tore her down. I had just graduated from college and Eric Bob and I decided to go down there and watch. I talked to this young lawyer who thought that there had to be a way this tragedy could be prevented from happening again."

"I guess that would be Joe."

"Exactly. After a while we couldn't watch anymore, so we all left, Eric Bob, me, Joe, and his strange friend named Steve. We started to discuss what we could have done to save the building. It was there that Joe introduced us to his plan. We were just young and stupid enough to go for it. Joe later introduced us to Ted and Ed, and the Travis Club was formed."

* * *

Taylor continued his narration on the sights of the city from their private vantage point for the next three hours. He pointed out the gargoyles below them on the Tower Life Building, which warded off the evil spirits that architects had thought would harm the early skyscrapers. He traced the River Walk from its beginning behind the old Municipal Auditorium through downtown into the King William District. He showed her the old armory that had been converted into a beautiful corporate campus.

He told the history of the Milam Building, the world's first totally air-conditioned skyscraper, and explained how the businessmen who first occupied the building had to be sold on the merits of "refrigerated air." Next, he directed her attention to the baroque Majestic Theater, the masterpiece of theater designer John Eberson. He told her how craftsmen, many with fathers who built the Majestic, lovingly restored her to her former glory.

He directed her eyes toward the Old Ursurline Academy that had been ready for the scrap heap until the Conservation Society decided to save it and convert it into a craft center. He told the story of the Old Lone Star Brewery, since converted into the San Antonio Museum of Art.

He pointed out La Villita, the oldest section of San Antonio, a former slum that was rebuilt by the WPA during the Depression into a beautiful village of small shops and restaurants. Next on the verbal tour came the Arneson River Theater, where the audience and the stage were separated by the waters of the San Antonio River and where barge tours brimming with visitors cruise through performances as if they were part of the show.

Minutes turned into hours, and night into dawn. As the sun's purple glow began to seep between the buildings, Logan realized why this man rarely dated. He was already in love.

"Can you explain some things to me?" Logan asked as the early sun reflected on the glass and steel of the newer buildings to the north. "Why do the city lights end so abruptly on the North Side?"

"An excellent observation," Taylor said, beaming. "Few people ever notice that when I bring them up here. Most of the growth in San Antonio is on the North Side. But, as you noticed, there are areas where the lights just end rather than flicker out. That's known as the recharge zone."

"Recharge zone?"

"You see, the city of San Antonio gets all its water from an aquifer, an underground lake so to speak. The city has no reservoir, and for that matter, no water treatment plants, because it has some of the purest water in the world."

"Anyway, this aquifer, the Edwards Aquifer, is a very mysterious body of water. Nobody knows how much it actually holds. Some experts feel that the aquifer is vast and the city needs no other water supply.

Others feel that we have reached the limit and need to start building a system of reservoirs just in case we do suck the whole thing dry. Of course, there are those who say that the pro-reservoir forces merely want to replace the aquifer as the city's water supply so it can continue to push development northward over the aquifer's recharge zone. Right now, that land is off-limits to any type of development that might contaminate water, such as gas stations, factories, golf courses that use pesticides, or large subdivisions with huge septic needs. About the only thing that land is good for is dry land ranching. So basically, the land is of little value because it can't be developed."

"Do you ever have a short answer?" she said, smiling.

"You asked," he shot back.

"So, what do you believe, Mr. San Antonio?"

"I don't know what to believe, but I, like most people in the city, feel that the aquifer is a precious resource, and that even if it is not limited, we should be careful what we build over the recharge zone. We can't take the chance of ruining it forever."

"Dat is right, Mr. Nichols," came the booming voice from the bathroom window. "And you promised me that you would be out before light. Now poor Karl Guenther will face ze wrath of his superiors. Out, Out, OUT! It is time to go. Now!"

"I'm sorry, Karl, I lost track of time—"

"Go, Go, Go. It is time for me to go home. Which, by the way, Mr. Nichols, you vill be visiting soon with your friends. And the lovely lady will be joining you to see my beautiful Hill Country ranch."

"You own a Hill Country ranch?" queried an impressed Logan.

"100 acres of the driest scrub land you'd ever want to see," said the straight-faced Taylor.

"Driest scrub? I happen to have a very nice well and all the free water I want from the aquifer. Laugh all you want, but you better come soon, because the time is coming when old Karl sells the Guenther homestead and moves into the city."

"You've been saying that for years, Karl. You'll never sell; that has been in your family for years. Your relatives would kill you."

"Yes, they would be quite mad at old Karl Guenther, but I'm the one stuck there. If they want it, they can buy it from me."

"That'll be the day."

"Go now, Mr. Nichols; I have grown tired and am ready to go home. You have overstayed your welcome. Besides, we would all die if we waited for you to kiss this girl."

Chapter 5

Alta Vista was not the typical San Antonio neighborhood. To the east stood the historic mansions of Monte Vista. Built by cattle barons in the early part of the century, these majestic homes were once the haven for San Antonio's rich and beautiful.

Beacon Hill rose to the west. Despite the tony moniker, it hardly resembled the Boston neighborhood that shared its name. At one time, middle-class white families had populated the Hill, but now most of them had moved to North Side suburbs and Hispanic families had taken their places.

Stuck in the middle was Alta Vista, always in the shadow of the historic district to the east. Few San Antonians had ever even heard of the neighborhood. Its cozy apartments and cottages housed urban pioneers, students, gay men, poor families, and the elderly, all drawn by the low rents and easy access to downtown.

The neighborhood was an enigma. One block featured skillfully restored homes and quaint old apartment buildings, while the next brimmed with dilapidated dwellings sliced into cheap flats.

One hundred sixteen Lynwood Street had at one time been just another of the neighborhood's many nondescript residences. In 1927 a young civil engineer bought the two-story duplex for his new bride, Edna Floraman. Over the successive years, the couple took in numerous single men and small families as tenants, providing a nice side income. When the stock market crashed in 1929, however, the Floraman home changed forever. A young architect named Randall Hugley took residence there.

The Depression hit Hugley even harder than most. By then, his fast-rising reputation had earned him an impressive list of clients. The ribbon had scarcely been cut at his masterpiece, the Texas Theater, when the market crashed. Those who remember the grand old cinema said it truly was a work of art. But in early 1930, construction everywhere stopped as the financing dried up. Hugley's office suite closed and he went bankrupt. As luck would have it, Louis Floraman's Alta Vista apartment was vacant. Fancying himself as a poor man's patron of the arts, he let Hugley stay there for free. He knew of the man's brilliance and had long been an admirer of his work.

In return, Hugley remodeled the Floraman home with extra supplies that his landlord could bring home from the public works yard. Soon the once-sedate house bustled like an anthill. First, an extensive balcony and porch sprung up in the front. Then, they constructed a solid wood staircase between the two residences, modeled after the nail-less one at San José Mission.

Work was slow for the young architect during the early part of the Depression. But the Works Progress Administration provided new opportunities for Hugley and his contemporaries. In 1935 he got a job designing a flood control project that would transform the downtown portion on the San Antonio River into a park-like haven. At first, locals scoffed at his pipe dream of turning the trash-strewn river into the Venice of the Midwest, but the government asked fewer questions than local residents, and federal money flowed freely during the later 1930s.

Adjacent to the river project, Ed Floraman supervised another WPA job, the restoration of La Villita. A young architect named O'Neil Ford had been assigned the task of bringing back to life this run-down slum, the oldest settlement in San Antonio. Ford and Hugley became fast friends. Hugley took the role of mentor, teaching the importance of San Antonio's past, showing him the ancient missions on the South Side, and helping Ford understand the building's role in the city's history.

Before long, the Hugley apartment became a nocturnal gathering place for writers, artists and builders all employed by the government's Depression-era projects. The nighttime sessions soon evolved into a think tank for the city's creative community. It was also one of the few places in town one could get a beer. Every week Hugley and Ford would drive 30 miles north to New Braunfels to pick up a truckload of fine German bock. Ford had done some work in town and on these trips he gradually collected his compensation in ice and forbidden brew. Once, a treasury agent who attended one of the late-night sessions asked Hugley who the brewer was in the German town. The architect told him to check the Catholic Church. The shocked agent replied, "The church in New Braunfels is making beer?"

"No," replied Hugley; "It's the only place in town that's not."

The charismatic architect became a leader for his contemporaries. The young New Dealers flocked to him, and many had spent nights on his couch when money was scarce. It became quite noticeable that the downstairs neighbor's wife was also attracted to the handsome young architect. Soon there were whispers that the two were becoming a bit too close.

The gossip became too much for Mr. Floraman. In the summer of 1938, he sent his wife packing to his parents' house in Houston. Then he set in motion a plan to rid himself of Hugley forever. First, he turned the architect in to the city's inspector general. He produced document after document showing how Hugley had misappropriated materials for his own profit. He alerted the press to Hugley's use of government-owned equipment for private projects and the taxpayer money spent on lumber, paint and cement to remodel a private home. The fact that the home belonged to Floraman failed to reach the press. When this tidbit finally did leak, the jealous husband produced a tidy public statement: "Of course it was my home! How shocked do you think I was to find out that I was paying to have my home remodeled and then to discover that all the materials had been stolen from the city work yard?"

Hugley realized that he could not win this battle. He resigned quietly and left town late at night, never to be heard from again. The only thing found left in the apartment was his gray cat.

Nine months later, Mr. Floraman sent for his wife.

* * *

More than 50 years passed before another man occupied the unit upstairs. Louis Floraman refused to take a chance again with his wife's affections. The couple's duplex became home to nurses, widows, schoolteachers, or any other harmless, single female he could find as a tenant. When Louis Floraman died in 1968, Edna vowed that the next tenant would be a man.

Unfortunately, a widowed bookkeeper lived to the age of 88, and she resided upstairs for the next 20 years.

By the time a vacancy finally opened up, the neighborhood had changed. Alta Vista had become home to many more students after Trinity University moved nearby in the early 1960s. One of the first people to look at the vacant apartment was a young history major named Taylor Nichols. Oddly enough, he had no intention of leasing the flat. He was more interested in the life of Randall Hugley. The student was writing a paper on the architect's local work and wanted to include a paragraph or two on the Floraman house. What he had hoped would be a 15-minute walk-through turned into a four-hour stay. By early evening he had made plans to move out of the dormitory and into the upstairs apartment.

Immediately after graduation, he published his first book, *The Life and Times of Randall Hugley.* The book featured rare drawings and photos of some of Hugley's most famous work, which Taylor had unwittingly found hidden in the attic of his apartment. One afternoon, while changing a bulb in his bedroom closet, he noticed that thin cracks seemed to trace the outline of a panel on the ceiling. Upon pushing it up, he discovered tube upon tube of Hugley's drawings and blueprints, all carefully sealed and preserved.

For the first time, the people of San Antonio saw some of the original concepts behind the River Walk, The Texas Theater, and other local monuments such as the Mexican Marketplace.

The book quickly became a local hit, and it was also the first of Taylor's to go into a second printing. This success inspired him to pen another work, *Urban Renewal in San Antonio: A History of Success and Failure.* His second offering was a bit too detailed for the general public and sold poorly. The publisher was about to drop it when one of Taylor's old professors at Trinity made it required reading for his Urban Studies class. Soon the book was picked up by campuses all across America. His publisher, Kirk Dooley of Maverick Press in Dallas, sensed a goldmine and signed Nichols to a contract for 10 more books.

* * *

The phone continued to ring as Taylor fumbled with the keys. Mr. Tibbs lay perched at the door, ready to make his escape.

"Your phone is ringing!"

"I hear it, Mrs. Floraman."

"How did your date go last night?"

"It was great," yelled back Logan to a surprised landlady.

"Did he take you to the rooftop?" she yelled back. Their conversation continued as Taylor swung open the door and raced to the phone. Mr. Tibbs seized the opportunity to run outside, only to be quickly captured by Logan.

"Hello, this is Taylor."

"Taylor, It's Kirk Dooley, your publisher; remember me? Where have you been? For Christ's sake, big guy, I've been calling all night. You need to get a cellular phone."

"Those are for the rich man."

"Where have you been?"

"I had a date."

"Yeah, right."

"Kirk, I'm telling you the truth." He handed the phone to Logan and coaxed her to say hello.

The two laughed on the phone for a moment as Taylor quickly figured out that they were comparing his idiosyncrasies. "Yes, he did take me to the rooftop," she said, then handed the phone back to Taylor. "Why does everybody ask me that?"

He smirked uncomfortably as he grabbed the phone. "Anything this man told you is a complete lie. What did you tell her, Kirk?"

"I invited her to your book premier Thursday night. Write this down. Eight p.m. at the Fig Tree bookstore in Alamo Heights. Talk it up big today on your radio show. We want a huge crowd. *Alamo Secrets* is going to be a big hit. I've got book reviewers coming from the newspaper and *Texas Monthly* magazine. All three TV stations will be there. This could be your biggest one yet. And please, don't get arrested before Thursday.

The last thing we need is a story about you being chained to a toilet."

"Relax, Kirk; a little controversy is good for sales."

"Of course it is, which reminds me, the Catholic Diocese is a bit concerned about the chapters you wrote on Davy Crockett's tomb in the Cathedral."

"Concerned?"

"Did I say concerned? I meant pissed! Really pissed. Boy, are they mad. They want to see you before the book is released. Listen, Taylor, I know that a controversy can mean a lot of sales, but be careful. This is the goddamn Catholic Church we're talking about. We don't want this to become one of those 'banned in Boston' things. That may fly in Dallas, but it's death in San Antonio!"

"Nice word choice," chastised the author.

"You know what I mean, Taylor. I get a call from the freaking assistant to the bishop, a Father Olivares. He wants to talk with you as soon as possible. I'm warning you, big guy, a few thousand books aren't worth eternal damnation," he said laughingly.

"I'll call the good father and put on the silk gloves. I hope you didn't subject the pastor to your vernacular."

"Give me a break, Taylor," Kirk chuckled. "Listen, I'll be in town Thursday afternoon for the signing. This is an important one. I'm talking tie and coat, big guy. And tell your ragtag friends that for once, Salvation Army chic is not in. And for Christ's sake, tell your buddy to park his tacomobile in the back."

"Anything else, Kirk? I'm still on this date, remember?"

"Yeah, a couple of things. Good news first. Your book on Randall Hugley finally went into the third printing. It should be on the store shelves now. Congratulations. Second, I need those rewrites for your *Urban Renewal* book. We're going into the fourth printing and the updates need to be in ASAP. And if you have anything yet on the next book, I'd like to see it. I'm tired of the big secret. Can't you just tell me what it's about?"

"It's about water and its relationship to San Antonio," said Taylor.

"Water?! Jesus Christ, Taylor, nobody wants to read a book about water. You're going to send me to a pauper's grave. For Christ's sake, can't you write about interesting stuff?"

"Can't you write about interesting stuff?" What kind of comment was that, Taylor thought. What did Hemingway's publisher tell him, "An old man on a fishing boat? Can't you make it a young, good-looking guy and try to hook some female readers?"

Taylor finished his conversation, pushed Mr. Tibbs off the cord and replaced the phone.

Logan could see the creases in his brow as he walked away from his desk. He mumbled something about a quick shower before breakfast. After 24 hours of being awake, she finally realized how tired she was as she took off her shoes and stretched out on the old sofa. The place may not have been a candidate for *Better Homes and Gardens*, but it certainly was comfortable. Sparsely furnished, it looked like a mixture of garage sale chic and artist loft. She flipped on the TV and caught an early local news program. Her heavy lids soon sprang up, however, when the newscaster mentioned the Finck building.

"Last night, one of San Antonio's most historic buildings was saved from arsonists when police arrived in time to prevent local gang members from burning down the old Finck Cigar Factory. The building's present owner, developer Noel Black, was at the scene after the arsonists were arrested:

The camera cut to Black.

'I got a call from the police that some vandals were camped out in the Finck building with gas cans. Their intent I can only guess. I do not know why anyone would want to destroy this historic structure. Luckily, I was able to get here in time and catch the arsonists before they completed their evil.'"

Taylor came out of the shower draped in a towel.

"You just missed your story, Taylor."

"I'm sure it was well-balanced."

"They said that you were a bunch of arsonists. I don't understand. I saw the guy from Channel 5 do the story last night ... how did it get all changed around?"

"Like I said, Russell Rhodes filed the story, but someone made a call to the station and had it edited. It happens all the time."

Taylor stood watching the television for a moment. Logan couldn't help but notice his taut young body covered by only a towel. "How long have I spent with this man?" she thought to herself. "12 hours? Is he ever going to make his move? This guy sure works slow."

Chapter 6

The club gathered around one of the beat-up picnic tables on the restaurant's patio. The Guenther brothers quickly grabbed the best seats for viewing the miraculous Butter Krust bakery sign across San Pedro Street that continuously dumped out slices of bread from a mechanical loaf. Between them, they shared six bean and cheese tacos, the 1990s staple of San Antonio's young and poor.

Eric Bob Kaufman King grabbed the other seat with a bread sign vista and peeled the foil from two chorizo and egg tacos. Logan tried not to stare at their plates, which seemed so foreign compared with the Mexican food she knew. In front of her sat the dish of steaming carne guisada that Taylor had insisted she order.

Joe ordered a piping hot bowl of menudo, while Steve, fooling nobody, claimed he was not hungry. Joe, as usual, offered his tortillas. Steve then filled them with a heaping supply of pico de gallo, offered free to the diners. "Ah, the Travis Club special; the poor man's taco," chortled Steve, as he took a bite of his breakfast.

"Can I ask you people what the hell we're eating?" said Logan. "I went to school in Austin and I thought I knew Mexican food. What is this stuff?"

"People from Austin ... I laugh at people from Austin," rasped Joe in a mock bandito voice. "You get someone from God knows where, he eats his first enchilada that didn't come from a can, and he thinks he knows Mexican food. Ladies and gentlemen of the jury, I submit the following exhibits for your consideration: Exhibit A: this plate of carne guisada, the first plate ever sampled by the defendant. Exhibit B: This fine bowl of menudo, and Exhibit C, Eric Bob's delicious breakfast taco. Ms. Pierce, let me ask, what is the main ingredient of menudo?"

Logan looked the bowl of soup he pushed toward her and took a spoonful. Her curious smile quickly turned to a grimace. "Ew ... ummmm ... fat."

The guys howled with laughter as she spit her mouthful clumsily into a napkin and reached for a sip of water. "That, my lady, is not fat, but the finest cut of tripe available in San Antonio." Logan's faced paled with nausea as the laughter intensified. The surrounding tables chuckled also as the familiar joke played out.

Steve slammed down his hand and shouted, "I sentence you, Austinite, to 1000 lengua tacos."

"I am not an Austinite; I'm from Dallas."

"Even worse! I add on an additional 1000 chicarrón tacos." The whole restaurant was now laughing.

One of the ladies came from behind the counter and pulled Joe's ear. "José Reyes, you should be ashamed. Is this any way to treat a guest in my restaurant? Young lady, let me fix you a couple of eggs any way you like. You boys don't come back to my restaurant until you learn some manners."

The guys hung their heads low in shame as the whole restaurant now laughed at their expense. Finally, Eric Bob broke the tension by asking Logan the question of the morning. "So, did you visit the rooftop last night?"

"Why is everybody asking me that?"

The crowd howled as Taylor hid his embarrassment. "Can we get down to some serious business?" the author asked meekly as he tried in vain to change the subject.

"Business. Yes, business, let's get down to business," Joe said. I'm going broke buying chains and locks. Maybe someone else can buy them next time."

Eric Bob stared at the Butter Krust bread sign; the Guenther brothers fiddled with their napkins. Steve momentarily put down his taco to distance himself from Joe's generosity. "Maybe we could use rope. Rope would be cheaper than a chain."

"Rope?" laughed Joe. "You guys are going to send to me to the poorhouse in Steve's taco car."

More laughter followed. Once again, the taco car was both a source of pride and humor for the club.

"Laugh all you want at my wheels," Steve said defensively. "But, who offered to give Joe a ride downtown to Saturday court?"

"Of course, he forgets to mention that as soon as we find a judge to extend the ordinance on the Finck building, Steve pulls out a stack of parking tickets that he wants me to get dismissed."

"The taco car is a commercial vehicle," Steve said. "Therefore, I should be able to park it in areas that are so designated."

"Speaking of the taco car, you guys are all invited to my book signing on Thursday at the Fig Tree bookstore, but my publisher asked that Steve park his infamous wheels behind the store." Even Logan could not hold back her laughter now.

"Oh, he has the gall to ask me to park behind the store, but watch him ask me to lend him a coat and tie," said Steve in mock offense.

"Well, as long as you mention it, I do need that and a white shirt, if you don't mind."

"Oh sure, you'll wear my clothes to your signing but you won't ride in my car. I know where I stand with you." The whole restaurant was once again laughing with the club. Suddenly, the lady from behind the counter delivered Logan a more conventional breakfast and then grabbed Steve's ear.

"While you're at it, I don't want that giant taco parked in front of my business either. It makes the whole place look bad. Besides, it says Big Ern's Taco Palace on the side. The last thing I need is to give that guy free advertising."

Everyone present was now howling at Steve. But he remained unfazed; the taco car had brought him fame, albeit fame San Antonio style. "Taylor, I can lend you a shirt and tie, but I will not park out back. The taco car is a living, breathing entity. I could not hide the taco so much as I could hide the nose on my face. I drive the taco car; therefore I am the taco car."

"Then could you come late when there aren't any parking places left anyway?" quipped Taylor, who knew he was asking for too much. "Seriously, though, this is a big deal, so dress nice, guys. Oh, and by the way, anybody who reads my book will be banished to hell, but besides that be there at seven."

Joe's ears perked up. "What was that about being banished to hell?"

"Oh, the archbishop is a bit miffed about the section on Davy Crockett's tomb. They've requested a meeting with me." Silence fell about the table. Even in San Antonio, where there was a Catholic church on every other corner, one did not meet with the archbishop every day. The Guenther brothers inched slowly away, Steve gazed out toward the taco car, and Joe and Eric Bob glanced at each other.

"*The* archbishop, the guy with the pointed hat, the guy at my confirmation, Bishop Santiago ... that bishop?" whispered Joe.

"No, one of his assistants, a Father Olivares or something like that. Listen, it's no big deal. They're just a little upset about one chapter. I'm not worried, so don't you guys be."

"Well, until this all boils over," said Steve, "I think it would be best if you didn't ride in the taco car. I wouldn't want lightning to hit it and knock off a plaster tomato." This time the laughter broke the tension.

"Don't worry about it. I don't want it to ruin Thursday night. This is going to be a big deal. *Texas*

Monthly is reviewing the book, the newspaper is sending a reporter, I've got a date,"—he winked toward Logan—"and Russell Rhodes said he would do a story on the release."

"Speaking of Russell, did anybody see his report on the news this morning? It was as if Noel Black edited the story himself," remarked Eric Bob. "Somebody must have made a call."

Chapter 7

"Line 5, George from Alamo Heights. You're on the air."

"Hey Taylor, enjoying the show today."

"Thanks, George."

"Listen, the reason I'm calling is because someone told me that if anybody could help me you could. When I was a kid we used to go to Playland Park. I went by there the other day and the place looked awful."

"It's sad isn't it, George? Here's a place where half of San Antonio took their first dates and now the park just sits there rusting away. It's been closed for about five years now and I haven't heard of any plans to redevelop it."

"The reason I called is that I noticed that the Rocket, that great old wooden roller coaster, was gone. Someone told me that the whole thing had been moved to another amusement park. Is this true?"

"George, my friend, it is true. The Rocket lives! It's at an amusement park in Pennsylvania. The place—I believe is called Knoebel's Grove—purchased the Rocket and had it moved there a few years ago. Thanks, friend."

Stewart, Line 4. You are on the air."

"Taylor Nichols, you old bird you, I hear you got a new book finally coming out." Taylor quickly recognized the voice as that of one of his most faithful listeners. "This wouldn't have anything to do with the Davy Crockett tomb in the back of the cathedral being a fake, would it?"

"Well, Stewart, as a matter of fact that particular tomb is mentioned in the book."

"Hooootttt tamale, baby!" laughed the old man. "Didn't I tell you that the tomb was a fraud? I bet you're causing quite a stir!"

It was moments like these that made Taylor truly appreciate his radio show. Stewart was a frequent caller who had lived in San Antonio for all his 70 years. He, like many others, had called before with tips and ideas that Taylor would research and often end up adding to his books. But Stewart's call about the tomb of Davy

Crockett in the San Fernando Cathedral was his biggest coup yet. It took him months to track down the information and it would have led to a dead end if the Guenther boys had not found a long-lost book published by the Catholic Church that tried to cover up the fraud. It seemed that the old man had a knack of pointing him in the right direction. "Stewart, I am eternally in your debt. My new book, *Alamo Secrets*, comes out this Thursday, and if it weren't for you I could have never written it."

"You ol' dog you, I can't wait to read it ... "

"We are having a little signing party Thursday night at the Fig Tree bookstore in Alamo Heights and the public is invited. I would love for you to come."

"Well, that's a very gracious invite. I was supposed to have the Queen of England over Thursday, but she will have to wait," cackled the old man. "I must ask you, son, because I'm sure that you are, but are you working already on your next book and do you need any help from the ol' codger?"

"Well, as a matter of fact I am researching the background on a book about water and its relationship with the city."

"Very good, son, very good! The River Walk, the ancient acequia, the old Spanish aqueduct, the aquifer, George Brackenridge setting up the city's first public water system ... a lot of stories out there."

"Sometimes I wonder why you don't write these books, Stewart?"

"Because I'm an old man; I don't know nothing about spellin', or writin'! I only finished the sixth grade. I worked for a living," he snorted. "Listen, son, if I may suggest something. During the Depression, the city had planned to build a reservoir. The deal was set and then, all of sudden, the whole idea was dropped. I think if you looked into that you would find a very interesting story."

"Very interesting. The reservoir debate has been going for 60 years, right?"

"Yes indeed, but why build a reservoir when you have an underground water system called the Edwards

Aquifer and you can pump all the water you want for free?"

Stewart spoke the truth. San Antonio was blessed with a seemingly endless supply of pure water. The city had no reservoirs and needed no water treatment plants. The Edwards Aquifer supplied so much water that anybody was allowed to pump out as much as he or she wanted. Taylor had thought it was only recently that people had become concerned about the limits of the supply.

"Son, I can't wait to read what you uncover."

"As always, Stewart, thanks for the tip! You don't know how much you've already helped." He paused for a second and looked at the clock. "We need to take a short break; we'll be back after the news. I'm Taylor Nichols and this is San Antonio Uncovered on WOAI radio."

He looked through the double-paned glass and saw his ever-faithful producer Eric Bob work his magic over the controls and deftly toss the ball to newsman Bob Guthrie.

"Eric Bob, is Stewart still on the line?"

"Nope, he hung up as usual."

Stewart always hung up too soon. Taylor wished for nothing more than to spend a whole day with the man. His mind was sharp and his memories vivid. The stories he could tell!

But this morning Taylor's mind was not sharp. He needed the five-minute break during the news. He usually took this time to walk outside the control and stretch his legs. But today, he was too tired to move from the chair. He couldn't remember the last time he slept. Was it Thursday night? He remembered leaving Logan asleep on his couch as he left for the radio station. 'What a joke!' he thought to himself. Here was this gorgeous woman asleep on his couch, and he hadn't even kissed her yet. All he did was take her to the rooftop, but he took everybody there. It was just a big joke with his friends. Even Logan quickly realized that.

One more hour to go, he thought. He really didn't mind, though; he lived for these three hours every

Saturday. Even though he could have earned a more princely sum making tacos, he considered himself lucky to get the show, thanks in part to the fact that the host of the cooking program that previously held the time slot had changed his name from Jerry to Judy.

The skittish radio programmer gave Taylor the job after the story of the host's transformation made front-page news.

From the first day, the response from listeners was overwhelming. The phone lines were jammed for three hours. Everybody wanted to know what had happened to old Mission Stadium or what became of Captain Gus from the ancient Channel 4 afternoon kiddie show.

After his first day, the station signed him up with a two-year contract. Unlike his publisher, WOAI never regretted the move. They paid the eager author peanuts and profited nicely on advertising. And every Saturday morning, there was Eric Bob working an extra shift, guiding him through the show.

Taylor closed his eyes and wondered again how much sleep he had gotten the previous night.

"Hello, Eric Bob Kaufman King," he said through the intercom into the control room. "Are you as tired as I am?"

"I managed to get a few hours of sleep last night. Of course I didn't have a 'date' like you did. Were you a successful cruiser?" he said in a mocking tone.

"As successful as always!"

"Oh. Sorry to hear that, he laughed. "Hey, you may want to listen to the news. There are a couple of stories I bet you'll be interested in."

Taylor leaned forward and turned up the air monitor.

"... that's the second week of dry weather we have had and the aquifer continues to drop. Officials from the Edwards Underground Water District say that there is no need for concern; the aquifer water level is still at a safe level.

Developer Noel Black is in the news again. Last night the historic Finck building was saved from a band of arsonists. This morning, Black announced that he has decided to sell the onetime cigar factory to the

Brownstone Company from Dallas, which is reportedly considering converting it into apartments for the elderly.

Black also announced his acquisition of the St. Anthony Catholic Retreat just south of town. He bought the rarely used retreat from the Catholic Church and said he wants to preserve the building and turn it into a golf resort and business conference center.

Sports is next; we'll check out the Spurs, who had another big win last night ... "

"Did you hear that? Can you believe it?" shouted Taylor.

"I know, the Spurs won again! That's great!" quipped Eric Bob.

Taylor didn't acknowledge the joke. His mind raced over a thousand questions. Who or what is this Brownstone Company? Did last night's events force Black to sell? Did he realize that he was fighting a losing battle when it came to the Finck Building and decide to just cut his losses and get out? Taylor should have been elated that his cause had won, but instead he felt a cautious optimism. He had known Black too long to accept anything for face value.

"Thirty seconds until air time," shouted Eric Bob through the intercom.

And what was the deal with the St. Anthony Retreat? Even though the compound was designed by Randall Hugley, he knew very little about the place. While compiling information for his first book, the church had denied him access to the retreat. In fact, he could not think of anybody who had actually visited the place. The Catholic Church had always been very secretive when it came to that property. And now, out of the blue, it had been sold to Black. Why didn't any of this make sense?

"Ten Seconds, ten Seconds," screamed Eric Bob in a vain attempt to capture Taylor's attention.

And did Black really intend to preserve the retreat? He had heard that story before. Suddenly, his thoughts were rattled back to the present by a shoe hitting the glass that separated the control room and the studio.

"You're on!"

"Welcome back to San Antonio Uncovered on AM 1200, WOAI Radio. I'm Taylor Nichols and we go to Henry from the South Side."

"I heard in the news that Noel Black has decided to sell the Finck building. I was wondering what you thought about that."

"Henry, I'm more interested in what you think about it."

"Well, Taylor, I think it's a damn shame. Here is a man who wants to save a historic building in San Antonio, and the city cannot provide decent protection for his investment. I'm sure you heard the news about arsonists trying to destroy the old factory. I think it's sad that a man like Black who has added so much to this city has finally thrown in the towel. He's sending a message to everybody who wants to invest in our city, 'Hey it's not worth it.' I wonder if the people who provide the financing for such projects are going to look at this ... "

* * *

The shades on the window were drawn tightly to keep the midday sun from illuminating the office. A dark figure reached toward the radio and turned it off.

"Nice story. Who did you get to make the call?"

"A friend of mine from Dallas."

"'Henry,' what a great name. People in this town love the name 'Henry.'"

"What's our next move?"

"You keep watching him and find out what he knows. See if you can get into his files. We might need to plan a break in."

"You're the boss, Noel."

Chapter 8

Joe always said that you couldn't swing a dead cat in San Antonio without hitting someone who was either Catholic or in the Air Force. It was just a fact of life. The church had a living, breathing presence in this town. From Lynwood Street, Taylor could walk to three different parishes. The closest, Our Lady of Grace, was also known as Our Lady of the Cadillac because of the number of well-off worshipers from Monte Vista; to the north sat St. John's and to the west St. Agnes.

Locals often said that the only Anglos who ever attended the predominately Hispanic St. Agnes were those who wanted to escape the judgmental eyes of Our Lady of Grace. Taylor first visited the church while writing *Old Places, New Uses: A Look at San Antonio's Refurbished Treasures.* The church had converted an old neighborhood theater into a gymnasium for the St. Agnes School. He met Father Patrick there for the first time.

Father Patrick took an immediate liking to the young author, but then the priest took an immediate liking to anyone who recognized the genius of his remodeling job. The two further cemented their friendship when the Travis Club was sentenced to 250 hours of community service and the guys served their time by running St. Agnes' Catholic Youth Association basketball program. The idea came from the Guenther brothers, who had attended the school through the sixth grade.

Taylor rarely went to church anymore. In fact, he used to joke with his friends that he was a retired Catholic, which meant he missed mass on Sundays and could use a condom. But, it was a special Catholic condom with a hole in the end that you could only get from the bishop. Ted and Ed Guenther considered it blasphemous, and therefore were quite shocked when Taylor slid into the pew next to them that Sunday morning.

The Guenther brothers sat alongside their father and their mother Lupita, who was in her late 40s but still was quite striking. Lupita winked at Taylor as he took his seat and whispered, "I heard you had a date." His social life was always of interest to her.

In the pew behind them sat their Uncle Karl and his oversized family of grown kids and grandchildren. Even though Karl lived on the old family farm on the edge of town, he still made the weekly trek to St. Agnes and his nightly trek to guard the Tower Life Building. An old adage around the parish was that mass would not start on Sunday until the Guenther family arrived. Indeed, they helped pack the place.

As Father Patrick commenced the service, Taylor quickly remembered why he rarely attended church anymore. His mind began to drift as it usually did during mass. He remembered returning home from the station the day before to find no sign of Logan. He should call her, he thought. His mother always told him a man should call a woman after he took her out. That was part of his problem. Now in his 20s, he still took dating advice from his mother.

He thought about Noel Black selling the Finck Building and wondering what his true motives were. He wondered about the success of Alamo Secrets and whether it would finally be the big breakthrough he hoped for. And, he thought of his meeting the next day with Father Olivares. Who was this Father Olivares? And, if the bishop was so concerned, why was he delegating their meeting to some underling? His mind spun with questions, and he had come to the only man who could answer them: Father Patrick of St. Agnes Church.

As the mass concluded, Taylor lagged behind as the congregation funneled out and exchanged pleasantries with the pastor. A mostly Hispanic parish led by an Irish priest may have seemed odd anywhere else, but in San Antonio it was the norm. The Diocese filled its huge demand for clergy by bringing in most of its rank-and-file priests from Ireland. There was a time when even the bishop was Irish, but a minority of Hispanic priests had long since taken control of the church's upper hierarchy.

Taylor, at the end of the long line, finally shuffled into daylight and extended his hand to the priest.

"Taylor Nichols. What brings you to visit this humble parish only a few blocks from your house?"

"I need a little spiritual guidance," said Taylor, not troubling to conceal his smile.

"I listened to your show yesterday. Very entertaining."

"As was your sermon, Father."

"Your nodding head showed me how much you enjoyed it," said the priest wryly.

"Uuuhhh," fumbled the author, "I had a late night. Listen, can we talk in private?"

The priest led him back through the church and into the sanctuary, where he dismissed the altar boys.

"Would you rather talk in the confessional?"

"No, that's okay," said Taylor, the sarcasm not lost on him.

"Give me a moment, my son," the padre said as he lifted off his ceremonial robe to reveal a simple collared shirt. While Taylor waited, he walked over to a pair of unusual candlesticks made of a dark metal. Father Patrick had his back to him, but knew what Taylor had picked up. "Interesting piece, wouldn't you say?"

"Very. It almost looks as if they were made from the barrel of a rifle."

"Quite perceptive. That's exactly what they are. They were a gift from the late Bishop O'Malley. The guns were removed from the chapel at the Alamo after the battle and crafted into a variety of instruments, literally turning guns into plowshares. These were presented to the priest at San Fernando, who eventually gave them to the Diocese. I'm sure the new bishop would love to have them back."

"I can imagine. The church still feels it has a right to the Alamo. I bet any relics from the place are highly treasured."

The priest finished hanging his robe and turned to Taylor. "Well then, what does bring you to St. Agnes this fine Sunday morning?"

"Many reasons. I wanted to make sure you were going to be at my book signing party Thursday night."

"Yes, indeed; I got an invitation from your publisher yesterday. I wouldn't miss it for the world. It's the talk of the Diocese."

"Apparently so. In fact, I have been asked to meet with the bishop's personal assistant tomorrow, a Father Olivares."

"Father Olivares? Really?"

"You know this man?"

"Everybody knows Father Olivares. Some say that he is being groomed to be the next bishop. Others call him an opportunistic wolf in shepherd's clothing"

"Does it surprise you that I've caused such a controversy?"

"No. Your revelations on the Alamo have really caused a stir among the church's hierarchy. They are quite upset. No; I'm only surprised that you're meeting with Father Olivares."

"Why is that?"

Father Patrick scratched his chin and gathered his thoughts for a moment. "I have some suspicions."

"Suspicions?"

"Yes, that the church is interested in your work. All of your work, past and present."

"I'm sorry Father, but you've lost me."

"Don't get me wrong, Taylor; they are mighty upset with you, or at least with your new book, which from what I understand practically calls the Diocese a pack of liars."

"Well, I just presented the facts. I let the reader decide."

"Yes, you let the reader decide if the tomb in the back of the cathedral, which is visited by thousands of tourists a year who dump a lot of money into the collection basket, is really just a hoax."

"Well, when you put it that way you make it sound really bad."

The pastor chuckled. "As bad as it seems, I have a feeling the bishop's assistant wants to see you for a variety of reasons. I would ask you to do me a favor; would you come and visit me again and tell me the details of your meeting?"

"Sure Father; I'll drop by tomorrow."

"Do me one more favor. When you do come back, come during confessions. Act as if you are here to receive penance, wait in line like everybody else, and talk to me from the confines of the confessional."

"Why is that?"

"Because you were followed here."

"Followed?" Taylor walked toward the door of the rectory and looked into the chapel. "Followed by whom?"

"Merced." The priest lowered his tone. "The evil Merced."

"The evil Merced? That sounds like something from a horror flick."

"The church keeps a private investigator, Mr. Merced. This morning I saw him enter the chapel right after you."

"The church has a private investigator? Damn, you guys take this penance thing pretty seriously. What does this guy do, stand over your shoulder and make sure I say all my Hail Marys?"

The priest was not amused. "Hardly. The church mainly uses him if a priest is suspected on some type of damaging behavior: seeing a woman, hanging out in gay bars, child molestation. He is the bishop's own personal SWAT team. If a priest sees Merced show up at his mass, he knows the church is on to him."

"How do you know this guy was following me?"

"Let's just say, I live my life above reproach. I know he wasn't here for me. Besides, he came in right after you. And you're the only one of my parishioners who has called the Diocese a bunch of liars."

Chapter 9

The Truth About Davy Crockett's Tomb

"In the rear of San Fernando Cathedral is a tomb that supposedly contains the remains of Davy Crockett, James Bowie, William Travis, and the other heroes of the Alamo. A controversy that started more than 100 years ago about the contents of the tomb has mostly been forgotten, and tourists who visit the cathedral take it for granted that this is the final resting place of Davy Crockett.

The controversy started in 1889, when Colonel Juan Seguin wrote a letter stating that 50 years earlier he had taken the remains of the Alamo heroes and buried them beneath the altar of San Fernando Cathedral. Most people dismissed the letter until almost another 50 years later, when on July 28, 1936, workmen digging a foundation for a new altar at the cathedral discovered charred human remains. Excitement grew as church officials realized the importance of their discovery. The remains were exhumed with a variety of witnesses on hand, including Bishop L. O'Malley, Architect Robert Hugman, Mayor C. K. Quin, Adina DeZavala, granddaughter of Lorenzo DeZavala, and Mrs. Leita Small, caretaker of the Alamo. The remains were placed on public display for a year, then entombed on May 11, 1938. To quell rumors surrounding the findings, the diocese published a now-rare book entitled *The Truth About the Burial of the Remains of the Alamo Heroes.*

However, today some questions still remain on whether Davy Crockett is actually buried there. Most likely he is not. First of all, Santa Anna ordered the cremation of all the bodies left at the Alamo. Most likely, Mexican and Texan soldiers were buried together. Second, Seguin did not return to the Alamo until after the Battle of San Jacinto almost a month later. There is an excellent argument that the remains are those of the Alamo defenders; nevertheless, it would be a bit presumptuous to assume that they are the actual remains of Davy Crockett and some of his most famous comrades."

From the book *Alamo Secrets* by Taylor Nichols

Taylor dreaded this. As he sat in the reception area at the diocese office he could not help but think how poorly prepared he was for this meeting. Perhaps he should have brought Joe with him, telling the good

Father Olivares that he would not answer any questions unless he spoke to his counsel. Maybe he should have brought Father Patrick along. "Excuse me, Father Olivares. Have you met my parish priest?" That may have been a good idea, but Father Patrick had hinted that his presence would have just made it worse.

He should have at least dressed up a bit more. His jeans and Trinity University t-shirt now seemed inappropriate. Taylor was constantly underdressing, but then again, no one expected much from a guy who has to borrow a Salvation Army shirt from a friend for his own book signing.

The minutes ticked away as Taylor continued to wait. He had half a mind to walk out. After all, this was just a courtesy call. The church had no legal claim. Everything he printed was substantiated. They had no right to be mad at him for exposing the fallacy of the tomb. They should not have started the myth in the first place. He had only come to please his publisher, and now was beginning to resent it. They were probably in the next room laughing at him, watching him squirm. He half expected an overzealous nun to come out yelling, "Young man, Father Olivares will see you NOW!"

"Mr. Nichols, my humblest apologies for making you wait so long." Taylor started slightly at the voice behind him. He immediately noticed the priest's youth. He could have passed for a corporate junior vice president rather than a man of the cloth.

"I'm Father Olivares," he continued. "Thank you so much for coming to see us today. I half expected you to be gone after waiting for so long, and I wouldn't have blamed you if you had. We've been on a conference call with Rome all morning. As you know, the pope is planning another tour of the United States and we are working to bring him to San Antonio. The problem is coming up with the money. I tell you, it would be really exciting if he came here."

The priest gushed with excitement. It was obvious that Taylor's book had been pushed to the back burner. He led Taylor from office to office, looking for a place to meet, ruling out one after another, saying that someone would be using the space later. Finally Father

Olivares led the way into a conference room and shut the door.

"Can I get you anything? Coffee, soda water?" Taylor just shook his head no. "I appreciate you taking the time to come visit us. I know that your schedule must be quite busy with your book coming out Thursday."

"Well, I managed to fit it in. I thought this was important," said Taylor, dropping his guard just a bit.

"I guess you are aware of why we asked you here. We have heard that your new book has a chapter concerning Davy Crockett's tomb in San Fernando's Cathedral. I know that the book is not due out for a few more days, but you wouldn't have an advance copy for us to look at?"

"As a matter of fact, I did bring a copy of the chapter from the printing proofs. I hope you understand that everything I have written can be backed up with the proper documentation. Everything is based on fact," he said as he handed over the papers.

"I am sure it is, Taylor. May I call you Taylor?" The priest took the papers and quickly glanced over them, barely reading. "Taylor, for years the church has debated the significance of the mentioned tomb. It has been years since the bones were discovered, years before any of the present members of the diocese came into power. In a way, your book is a blessing.

"I am going to be frank with you. The church is concerned that we will be placed in an embarrassing position, that this whole thing will become a media circus, and that we will look foolish. The last thing the bishop wants is to become part of some publicity stunt in order for you to sell books. I trust that is not your intent."

Taylor was clearly taken for a loop. Embarrassing the church was the last thing on his mind. He just happened to come across another interesting 'only in San Antonio' tale and he just wanted to write about it.

"No, that was never my intent."

"I never thought it was. To be honest, Taylor, I've been a big fan of yours for quite some time. I listen to your show quite often and I have many of your books. I am particularly interested in your book on Randall Hugley."

The young writer was totally taken aback. He had come ready for a battle and now he felt as if he was going to be asked to sign a book.

Father Olivares continued, "I've always admired his work. Did you know that when he created the River Walk, he designed every staircase that led down to the river level differently? Amazing when you consider the number and the detail in each one."

Of course Taylor realized it. He wrote it.

"I was reading your book on Hugley the other day. You have amazing insight into his work. I've never seen an architect who designed so many hidden doors and passageways."

It was true. Even Taylor's apartment, which had been remodeled by Hugley, had a hidden door he discovered while in college. It was behind that door that he found the architect's stash of drawings.

"I'm sure you realize that Hugley designed the St. Anthony Catholic Retreat. I would consider it one of his more significant works, yet you practically ignored it in your book. Why was that?"

Taylor remembered quite well why he had written so little about that particular building. The church had denied him access to the property. Despite numerous calls and letters to the diocese the answer was always no, and never with an explanation. But in the spirit of goodwill that Father Olivares was showing him, he answered diplomatically, "Basically, it was a case of deadlines. I was running out of time and didn't get to include everything in the book that I wanted."

"I see. Such a shame; it really is a beautiful building. When you were writing your book, did you get to interview the man?"

"Unfortunately, no. Hugley left San Antonio under less than favorable conditions. He was discredited as an architect and lived in obscurity in California the rest of his life. From what I understand, he passed away some years ago in a nursing home."

"That's really a sin; I'm sure you would have enjoyed meeting him. I hear that you possess a large collection of his drawings?"

Taylor was starting to wonder if the good Father had ever really read his book. It was stated clearly how he had happened to come across his work. "Yes, I do."

"The reason I'm asking, Taylor, is that we need your help. I'm sure you have heard by now that the building and the land were sold recently to Noel Black. He has graciously allowed us to go back in and reclaim some church artifact—uh ... property—that was left behind. We have checked our archives and cannot find the blueprints anywhere. We were wondering if you had access to them."

Taylor already knew that he did not. He had catalogued every blueprint, note and scribble that Hugley had left behind. Everyone was carefully preserved and sealed in the attic where he had found them years earlier. "I really don't know what I have; there is so much. I would have to go through it again."

"Taylor, if you would do me a favor and look over those materials. If you could give a call in the next day or so I would appreciate it. I really need to find those drawings." The priest got up and opened the door, "Here's my card. Please don't hesitate to call."

Taylor got up to leave when the priest handed him a copy of his book. "If you don't mind, would you please sign a copy of my book? Like I said, I've been a big fan for a long time. I bet I was one of the first to buy your book."

Taylor took the book and left his autograph. Before he handed it back, he glanced at the publisher's code. This was a copy from the third printing and had only been on the shelf for a matter of days.

* * *

As soon as Taylor had been escorted out, the pastor returned to the conference room. The father opened a door that led to the bishop's office. The bishop was seated behind the receiving end of a two-way mirror.

He held out his hand for the father to kiss his ring and asked, "Do you think he has the blueprints?"

"I don't know. He might."

"How much do you think he knows?" asked the bishop.

"Right now, very little. But, we have taken a risk asking him to come here. We planted a seed of curiosity in his mind. He'll start digging around. He could be trouble in the future."

"You'd better keep an eye on him. Perhaps you should have Merced keep tabs on him."

Father Olivares stared out a window, avoiding his superior's eyes. "Perhaps ... that would be a good idea."

"With the pope planning to visit, this could be real trouble," the bishop said, raising his voice. "I will not allow some adolescent writer to be my downfall. If this gets out of hand, you'll be saying mass at a shanty town parish on the border."

* * *

Confessions were heard at 5:30 p.m. at St. Agnes. The weeknight sessions usually only drew the truly faithful. Taylor fidgeted as he waited in line. He could not remember the last time he had been to confession. Maybe it was in high school. Fifteen minutes passed before he finally got his chance to enter the tiny booth and wait for the priest to open the screen.

Taylor knelt on the small riser, wondering what the woman in the other booth was confessing. These were the people who came every week. 'Surely no one could accumulate that much sin in a week,' he thought to himself. 'Bless me, Father, but I used a cheaper brand of margarine in the cookies for the bake sale.'

His screen finally slid open and Taylor announced, "Welcome to McDonald's. May I take your order?"

"Hello, Taylor. I'm glad to see your first trip to confession since you stated shaving will be taken seriously," said Father Patrick. "Did you visit the diocese office?"

"I did, and you were right. They wanted me there for a totally different purpose. They wanted me to give them the blueprints—"

"To the St. Anthony Retreat."

Taylor recoiled silently in shock. "You knew."

"No, I suspected. And I was right. I was quite shocked when I heard that the church had sold the property, and even more shocked when I had heard who bought it. There have been a number of rumors surrounding that place for years."

"Rumors? Such as?"

"It would be best if I didn't say. It would be best if you didn't know."

"I don't understand."

"I know, but you must realize that all I have heard is rumor and hearsay. But it was the talk of the diocese when the news broke that the place had been sold. There have been some who say the place was sold months ago, and that the story was suppressed."

"What I don't get is why am I suddenly involved in this."

"They think you may know something."

"Know something!" he practically yelled before lowering his voice, remembering that he was in the confessional. "I don't know anything."

"You know more than you think you do, Taylor. You said they asked you if you had the plans to the retreat. Do you?"

"No, I don't. But I told them that I didn't know if I did, that the papers that I found were in such disarray that I didn't know what I had."

"Good."

"I figure if anybody can find the plans, I could. I know the county archives better than anyone."

"Of course you do. Let me give you a piece of advice. Play it cool. Hold off Father Olivares for as long as possible. Keep them in the dark. Don't let them realize what you know and don't know. The longer they wait, the better it is for you. "

"Better for me?" he said facetiously. "Am I in danger?"

"No, not in danger. But you have no idea what they really want from you. Keep them at bay; let them sweat."

"Sure, no problem," Taylor said sarcastically. "You're not the one being followed."

* * *

He knew that it was going to be a long night. That was the way his life seemed to work. Everything always happened at once. He had a book coming out on Thursday. He had started to see a girl, a woman really, with whom he really wanted to spend time. He had to finish the rewrites on *Urban Renewal* by Friday morning and continue research on his latest effort. And now, to top it off, he was getting dragged into something with the Catholic Church.

The way his life worked, his next week would be the complete opposite. Five days of nothing to do, lying around watching Cubs games on cable TV at Steve's house.

He needed to get off the couch and get to work, but he couldn't help thinking about his meeting with Father Olivares. He assumed it was he who had sent Merced to follow him. Was he standing outside watching him now?

As often was the case when time got hectic, he tried mentally to prepare a schedule for the upcoming week. First priority was to prepare the rewrites before his publisher left town on Friday morning. "Great," he thought to himself, "but before I do that, I need to go to the county archives and try to find those plans. And before I do that, I need to call Logan. I wonder if she is going to be mad because I haven't called. Maybe it would be better if I didn't call. Make her wonder; make her wait. Why should I be the one who calls? She hasn't called me either."

He continued to debate himself as he dialed her number.

Chapter 10

Tuesday mornings were rather quiet at the courthouse. The records department, hidden in the basement, often reeked of mildew and bat guano. "Welcome to the glamorous world of historical research," Taylor thought.

He was greeted by a young man who immediately recognized the author.

"Taylor Nichols! I had a feeling I would be seeing you soon."

"Mr. Meacham," Taylor replied with mock respect, "I have a special favor to ask of you."

"As always, I am at your service." Meacham knew that an acknowledgement at the end of Taylor's books always impressed his supervisors and did not hurt during raise time.

"I am looking for the blueprints for the St. Anthony Retreat. Do you think that you could find them for me?"

"No can do, Taylor."

The author mistook his tone as a joke. "I'm kind of in a hurry, Meacham; I don't really have time to goof around today."

"I'm serious, man, we don't have them."

"How can you know? You haven't even looked."

"Haven't looked? That's a laugh, man. That's all I've been doing for weeks. We seriously don't have them."

Taylor stood in disbelief. "The county has no building permit records?"

"No building permit records. No records with the historical preservation committee ... "

"How about the water board or City Public Service?"

"I'm telling you, man, I've been checking for weeks. I've looked everywhere, with everybody. I've even been to Austin. There is nothing, anywhere. They're all gone, not a trace of paper. As far as the state is concerned, that property doesn't even exist."

Taylor couldn't believe it. Gone. Vanished. Nothing left. He thought over and over about where else in the county those records could be filed, but he knew Meacham well enough to know that no stone had been left unturned. He had even been through the records maze in Austin. If there had been anything, Meacham would have found it.

"And I'll tell you the weird thing, Taylor. As far as I can tell, those blueprints and all the stuff from the building permit records have been missing for over 50 years."

Missing for 50 years? What had he stumbled into? Then, as he was ready to stalk out the door in disgust, it hit him like a ton of bricks. "Meacham, you said that you've been looking for weeks for these plans? Who else has been here?"

"Let me see," he said, opening his books. "About three weeks ago someone representing Noel Black Developments first requested the drawings. When I couldn't find them, he returned ... on ... Friday-no, Monday-asking me to look again. That following Tuesday, a Father Olivares came in asking for the same thing. Says he represented the bishop. That was exactly two weeks ago today. He got really mad when I told him I couldn't find them."

"Did you tell him that Black had already been there?"

"Yes, and that's what got him really mad, which was strange, because I noticed a transfer of the title from the local diocese to Black about 2 months before."

Taylor sat stunned. "That property was sold that long ago?"

"Yes, I know what you're thinking. They just announced the sale this weekend. Why the secrecy? This is what else is strange. The day after Father Olivares leaves, I get called upstairs into the County Commissioner's office. He calls me on to the carpet and tells me to get off my butt and find out those plans. That's when I started looking everywhere, the water board, the state. Believe me, man, there is nothing to be found. The only thing I can't figure out is who made the call upstairs, Black or the church."

* * *

Taylor left the courthouse with more questions than answers. He really had not expected the scene at the courthouse to unfold as it did. He figured that the church might have checked the archives for the drawings, but he thought he could dig them up through one of his other channels. His last resort was always to go to Austin, but Meacham had already been there. Maybe Meacham was lying, but that was unlikely. A simple phone call could verify if he had really checked the state archives. Deep down, he knew that was unnecessary.

Besides, he still had a trick or two up his sleeve. He had other places to search for information. He was not going to give up that easily. Stop number one: the Guenther Bookstore. As long as he was downtown, he might as well stop by later this afternoon. Looking at his watch, he realized that he could also zip on over to the bank and catch Logan for lunch. Taylor walked under the shade trees of Military Plaza and opened his wallet. The contents were slim. Lunch would have to be a Spartan affair.

A column of cool air hit him as he entered the bank, melting away his nervous sweat. He looked over to her desk, where her attention was focused on a computer screen.

"Would you want to give a guy a second chance on a car loan?" Taylor asked.

She looked up and a smile consumed her face. "Well, this is a surprise. What brings you back to the bank?"

"I was downtown doing research," he said, sitting down, "and I thought maybe I would take a break and see if you could go to lunch."

"Oh," she said, disappointed. "I've got to go to our South Side branch and meet with the loan manager. I guess that's the world of nine to five."

"I wouldn't know," said Taylor, shrugging. "I've never really fit into the corporate world."

"You would thrive in a world like this. Smart, attractive, self-motivated. You'd be surprised at how much you would like this type of environment. I really believe you would do quite well for yourself."

"Maybe I would; who knows?" said Taylor agreeably in an effort to change the subject. "All I know is that your corporate world has screwed up my lunch plans."

"I'm sorry," she sympathized. "Could I have a rain check?"

"Sure. Just name the place and time."

"How about tonight? After all, our date never officially ended. Last I recall, you left me asleep on your couch."

"Tonight would be great," he replied. "Why not let me make you dinner?"

"How could a girl resist a guy who can cook?"

"Well, I'll give it my best shot." As the two made their plans, Taylor could not help but notice how at ease he felt with her. She made everything so easy. They both got up as she escorted him out the back door. When they were out of view of the other bank employees, she kissed him on the cheek.

"See you tonight," she said before she turned to walk back inside. Taylor held his cheek and blushed as he turned.

* * *

The walk through downtown to the Guenther's bookstore was one of Taylor's favorites. He had made it hundreds of times. After spending a morning at the courthouse looking through old records, he would often take the River Walk past the Tower Life Building to the Presa Street Bridge, where he would pass the Hertzberg Circus Museum, turn left on Commerce Street at the original Alamo National Bank building, then enter the bookstore. He would often get there in time for lunch, only to find Mr. Guenther and his friends enjoying a *cerveza fria* while his sons manned the store. Today, however, was different.

Today was the beginning of the end of the Guenther family.

The shouting was so loud that those waiting for the bus at the corner could hear it. The thick German accents that amused the pedestrians told Taylor that Mr. Guenther and his brother Karl were the two combatants. Funny, thought Taylor; he had known the Guenthers for years, but it wasn't until today that he knew Mr. Guenther's name was Arthur. It had always been the formal Mr. Guenther. Unlike the friendly Karl, Mr. Guenther had always scared Taylor. For that matter, he scared Ted and Ed. Neither possessed the courage to tell their father that his bookstore was not their life's ambition.

Ted and Ed both stood by the front door, acting as though they were sheltering themselves from an invisible rain, hoping the people waiting for the bus would think that they did not work there. Taylor's appearance brought a momentary smile to their face.

"Welcome to World War III," quipped Ted.

"What's going on? I could hear your father screaming from the River Walk."

"It's bad, Taylor. It's bad. I knew this day was coming; I just hoped that I wasn't going to be around to see it. Uncle Karl sold the family ranch."

Chapter 11

In the back room of the bookstore, Karl and Arthur Guenther continued to joust. The ranch had been in their family for generations. The first Karl Guenther had come to San Antonio before the Civil War like the many other Germans who filled the towns of Fredricksburg, New Braunfels, and Kerrville. Karl Senior came from the lower Rhine, and had heard of Texas like the thousands of others who received letters from friends and relatives striking it rich in the new world.

Karl Guenther passed the ranch on to his oldest son, Karl Jr., who left it to his oldest son, Karl III. But, by the time Karl III took possession of the land, he had no interest in ranching. In fact, he had little interest in living on a piece of land that was nothing more than a flash flood waiting to happen. His sons and daughter all lived in town, as did his brother and his family. For years he threatened to sell the land and move into San Antonio, but was held back only by his brother, who felt that the property should stay in the family.

Karl III, now semi-retired, save for his continuing stint as a night watchman, had always believed he had little hope of ever selling the property. It sat over the aquifer recharge zone and therefore could never be fully developed. Even though it was now only a half hour from an ever-growing metropolis, it could never be more than a ranch as long as a city of a million people depended on the underground lake for their drinking water.

Ted and Ed spent years listening to the argument and wondered what implication it might have for them. They envied their cousins, who were not bound by traditions as they were. They longed for the day that they could escape the hold of their father and leave his musty bookstore. Now they wondered if they were about to be freed from at least one of these family responsibilities.

Taylor watched the concern in their faces and thought about something that Noel Black had once told him: "One man's history is another man's burden." For once in his life, Taylor agreed with Black.

Hoping to break the tension, Taylor blurted out his reason for the visit.

"I know this may not be the best time, but I need your help."

The Guenther boys had helped him many times in the past by finding old out-of-print books that aided his research or started an idea. "You know we are always glad to help. What are you looking for?" Ed said.

"I need to find out all I can about St. Anthony's Catholic Retreat."

"Oh yeah, the property that Black just bought. What do you have up your sleeve?" queried Ted.

"To be honest, I don't even know. I've been asked by the diocese to do some research for them, but I don't know why. I suspect that they haven't been totally honest with me."

"The diocese? So that's why you were in church on Sunday. You were going to meet with the bishop and you wanted to pick Father Patrick's brain before you went there," ventured Ed.

"Let me guess," said Ted, rubbing his head like a carnival fortune teller. "You already told the bishop that you had what he was looking for, and now you are hoping to find it."

"I'd love to stay and answer your questions, but I have a lot to take care of today."

"Oh, a date tonight with Logan?"

"A Taylor Nichols date? Going to make her pizza?"

"I've had enough of your mind reading. I'm leaving."

"Before you go," Ed whispered, rubbing his temples, pretending to intercept Taylor's thoughts, "I believe you are going to want this."

"What is it?"

"It's a copy of an out-of-print book from the thirties put out by City Public Service on the 100th year of water service in the city. I thought you may want it for your next book."

Taylor stared in wonderment at the Guenther brothers. "You guys are amazing."

Taylor walked toward the door, head buried in the book. As he stepped out of the shop, the argument once again rose in volume. He turned back toward the brothers and pointed, "Don't worry; at least you won't have to live on the ranch."

Taylor laughed and continued to the street. Before continuing he turned again toward the brothers. "You're not the only ones who can read minds."

* * *

Taylor fumbled with his keys as the phone rang. Mr. Tibbs waited by the door, hoping for an opportunity to escape and sensing that his owner was too preoccupied to pay attention. He finally had a chance to get outside, leaving his scent, marking his territory, keeping away the strays that often wandered up the back steps.

By the time Taylor could stumble inside with several bags of groceries, the answering machine had already picked up the phone. Deciding to monitor the call, he walked out to the back porch and scooped up his cat. He reentered to hear Father Olivares' voice over the speaker, leaving his phone number.

"In due time, Father," he said to no one in particular.

Taylor began to unpack the food. Cheese, pepperoni, tomato paste, cheap wine; all the ingredients for a perfect date. Having worked in college at a pizzeria, he was quite adept at tossing dough and creating both a show and a meal. While others entertained with backyard barbeques, Taylor preferred to recreate the atmosphere of Little Mike's Italian Palace in his kitchen.

He figured he had about 30 minutes before Logan arrived, and his usual pre-date jitters had yet to overtake him. But still he wondered. He had already taken her to the rooftop, and was about to make pizza for her. It had not even been a week and already he had used up most of his bag of tricks. What happened next was always a mystery to Taylor. At this point, his relationships tended to either take off or just die a quick death. Usually it was the latter.

He looked at the clock and jumped into the shower, and thought about his wardrobe options: a somewhat-new t-shirt that celebrated 100 years of Texas League baseball or a collared golf shirt with someone else's initials from the Salvation Army.

After pulling the golf shirt over his head, Taylor combed his hair and contemplated using some cologne that he got for graduation and now smelled more like alcohol than anything else. He heard a knock on the door just as he returned the unused bottle to the shelf.

"Hey beautiful," he said as he opened the door and stared at Joe, who was holding a bag and a six-pack of beer.

"I always knew that you thought of me that way," Joe said, smirking as he handed him the bag. "I brought you some mushrooms; you always forget the mushrooms when you make pizza."

"How did you know I was making pizza?"

"I stopped by Ted and Ed's this afternoon and they told me that you would probably forget the mushrooms tonight. Want a cold one?" Joe ripped off a can of Pearl

Beer and offered it him. "Heard you were on a little mission for the church."

"Yeah, I go down to the diocese headquarters yesterday expecting to get raked over the coals, but instead this Father Olivares tells me how great I am and barely asks about the book. Then he asks me to help him find the blueprints to the St. Anthony Retreat. He says that Noel Black has allowed them to go in and recover some artifacts, but they need something to go by."

Joe opened his own can of beer and walked out to the balcony, where he took a chair. "Sounds kind of fishy."

Taylor followed him out and took a seat on an old plastic milk crate. "You want to hear something really strange? I went to St. Agnes Sunday for mass and Father Patrick says I was followed—by some guy who works for the church."

Joe leaned forward. "Sounds like Merced."

"Merced! You know this guy?"

"Yeah. About a year ago I was asked to defend a teacher at a Catholic school who was accused of child molestation. Though it was obvious that the charges were baseless, the church wanted him out. They offered him a settlement where he could have resigned with a nice severance, but he declined. So the church brought out this Merced character, who had been compiling a volume worth of dirt. The poor guy didn't know what hit him."

"So why is a guy like this following me?" asked Taylor worriedly.

"I don't know. On one hand, you have the church asking you to find something for them. But on the other hand, you've got the church following you, probably searching into your background as we speak."

Taylor looked glumly at his beer. "Kind of sounds like they want me to find the key to their treasure chest, but are afraid I'll be around to open it."

The two sat in silence, hoping for a cool breeze. Taylor's worried eyes offered no protection for his thoughts.

"Boy, was World War III going at the Guenther Book Store or what?" asked Joe in an attempt to change the subject.

"Tell me about it. It was pretty heated when I was there," Taylor said, cracking a smile as he popped open another can. "You could hear them clear out in the street; people at the bus stop were checking it out."

"It iz not your decizion touse make," Joe mocked, imitating Karl Guenther. "Thank God he finally found a buyer; he'd be dead before Disney came knocking."

Taylor laughed at the Disney reference. For years Karl had been telling them that the Walt Disney Company was secretly buying land on the outskirts of San Antonio for a new theme park. Many people passionately believed this legend, retelling tales of how the Disney people had done the exact same thing in Orlando, buying the land through a third party. Taylor could never bring himself to tell Karl that he had heard the exact same rumor in over a dozen cities and the probabilities were low that a Texas Disney park would ever become a reality.

Their conversation was interrupted by a knock on the door, which reminded Taylor that he was waiting for a date. He opened the door to find Steve holding a white shirt, coat and tie. "Hey, is there a party going on?"

Joe tossed Steve a beer as he entered and handed the shirt to Taylor. "Here's the clothes I promised you for your book signing, along with a white shirt freshly laundered and pressed courtesy of the fine clothiers at the Salvation Army. What's the occasion here?" asked Steve as Taylor put the garments in the closet.

"I'm supposed to be on a date," Taylor said.

"Sorry," answered Steve, as he opened the beer and popped a slice of pepperoni in his mouth. "I didn't know that you and Joe had a thing going."

"Logan is supposed to be here any minute."

"Let me see, the rooftop on Friday, pizza on Tuesday. You sure do move fast." Once again, a knock on the door halted the conservation. Steve darted to the door, cutting off Taylor. "Hello beautiful!"

"Well Steve, I never knew you found me so attractive," joked a flattered Mrs. Floraman. "If I was 50 years younger, I'd show you a thing or two. Are you having a party up here tonight?"

"No, Mrs. Floraman; Taylor is supposed to be on a date."

"In my day, when a young man went on a date he usually didn't take his friends along."

"It wasn't supposed to happen this way," Taylor said pointedly. "Would you like something to drink? A beer, some wine?"

"I'll have some wine, but just a little. You know, Taylor, many years ago this old upstairs apartment was host to many impromptu parties." Her eyes glazed over as she remembered a younger self. Taylor, sensing the moment, handed her a wine glass and kissed her on the cheek.

"Please stay for a while; there will be plenty of food."

"I'll stay for bit. I just came up to tell you that you had a visitor earlier today. A young man, a Father

Olivares, stopped by today looking for you. You are not in some kind of trouble, are you?"

Joe quickly glanced up from the pizza that he began to make. "Father Olivares?"

Taylor tried to hide his concern but fooled nobody. "Yes, Mrs. Floraman. He wants me to do a favor. Seems that he needs information on the old St. Anthony Retreat."

Mrs. Floraman came back to the present when she heard the retreat mentioned. "The St. Anthony Retreat. Wasn't that designed by Randall Hugley?"

"Exactly. It seems like the former tenant of this apartment didn't leave the church any designs to the place, and they want me to supply them."

"And let me guess, you don't have them either," said Steve.

"Seems like no one does. I've been to the county, the state archives have been searched, and get this: both the church and Noel Black have been searching for them." Taylor looked at the faces that surrounded him.

The mention of Black's name made everybody look up at the same time. Even Mr. Tibbs walked into the room.

Joe reached down and petted the cat under his neck. "Isn't this a kick in the pants? Once again we're a thorn under Black's saddle, and now we don't even know why."

"That's the big question. Why is everybody so desperate to get these plans?" Taylor asked. A knock on the door ended the discussion.

"This had better be a woman," he said as he opened the door to reveal Logan, dressed in bright pants and a tailored shirt that most likely had not come from the racks of the Salvation Army Thrift Shop. She leaned over to kiss Taylor, when she noticed three sets of eyes and a cat watching her.

"I didn't know this was going to be a party," she whispered.

"I didn't know either. It just kind of happened." Taylor could not help but notice that she was beaming with excitement. "You look like the cat who swallowed the canary."

"I've got the greatest news," she announced as she walked into the apartment. "I had a meeting this afternoon with the president of the bank. They're looking for a new community affairs director. I told him about you and he was very excited. He wants to meet with you as soon as possible. Taylor, this job is yours if you want it!"

She looked around the room and noticed the look of shock in everybody's eyes. In the back of the room, Steve fought hard to suppress a laugh.

* * *

Steve, Joe, and Mrs. Floraman retreated to the kitchen as Logan and Taylor headed toward the balcony. Joe began to slice the mushrooms as Mrs. Floraman helped herself to another glass of wine. Steve craned his neck in a futile effort to hear the discussion out front. "Can you believe it? A job. She wants him to get a regular job!"

Joe looked up from the mushrooms and motioned with his head for Steve to stop his eavesdropping. "You know, Steve, 'job' is not a four letter word. They come in very handy when you need to pay bills."

"As Taylor's landlord, I would like to testify that he is not very timely with his rent check." Mrs. Floraman's blunt comment surprised the two as they realized that the wine was beginning to have an effect on her.

"But, a job like that?" questioned Steve, "A bag man for the suits at a bank? Taylor would hate that."

"How would you know?" Joe asked loudly, before checking the tone of his comments. "You've never had a real job in your life."

Steve took the remark as a compliment. "Exactly, and neither has Taylor. We're not those kinds of guys," he said, liberally comparing himself to the writer. "Taylor is the kind of guy who wants to hang out in the library all day then stay up until sunrise writing. Do you see a guy like that succeeding in the corporate world?"

"I see a guy like Taylor succeeding in anything he tries."

Steve pointed his finger at Joe as if he was making a point to a jury. "Yes, I agree; Taylor would be successful in such a job. But then I must ask you, what is your definition of success? Is it a well-paying job with enough money to buy the nicer things in life, or is it spending your time working at something you truly enjoy and love? I say that Taylor really loves his life's work now, and if he took a bank job he would have to give that up. It's not like he has a family to support. He doesn't have to take a job he doesn't want."

Mrs. Floraman refilled her glass and stared at the wall. "I loved two men in my life. One loved a job he couldn't do, and another hated a job he had to do."

Steve and Joe both looked at each other and realized that the elderly woman had had too much to drink.

* * *

Taylor woke up from the couch and looked at the clock. It was 10:30 in the morning. His mind was clouded from the boxed wine he had drunk into the wee hours. He went into the kitchen and discovered the remnants of a night filled with good food, cheap alcohol and great conversation.

He had never seen Mrs. Floraman drink so much, but then he had never seen her so happy. She acted like a young girl as she told stories about the parties they used to have in this apartment when Randall Hugley lived there. She told them about the night when he first revealed his thoughts on building the River Walk between the streets of downtown. She recounted tales about the number of artists and writers who stopped by to drink the cases of illegally-brewed German beer during prohibition. Taylor could easily tell that those were the happiest days of her life.

Then Taylor remembered his night with Logan and how he had to quickly usher her out to the balcony to shield her from the three pairs of shocked eyes. He promised to set up an appointment to visit with her boss on Friday, something he dreaded, but at least he would have a shirt to wear if the one he borrowed from Steve was still clean enough after Thursday night.

"Thursday night," he thought to himself. He had to have those rewrites done by then, tomorrow. He still wanted to go to the Alamo Library to do some research on the ancient acequia water system for his upcoming book. Not to mention that he had had a few more places to check before getting back with Father Olivares. He had two days before the signing party and enough work for an office full of grad students. He was sure glad he didn't have a job.

Chapter 12

Taylor had one hour to shower, shave, get dressed, and drive to the bookstore. Maybe he was cutting it close, but he had been at the library all day and had gotten on a roll there. He was confident that he had plenty of time. He ignored the phone, which seemed to ring constantly. Taylor was pretty much on schedule when he toweled off and reached for the shirt Steve had brought him.

Say what you want about Steve, he thought, but he always had a large supply of freshly laundered shirts from the Salvation Army. Taylor stood in front of the mirror and put on the shirt and tie Steve had chosen for him. As he tucked it in, however, he noticed something wrong. Something horribly wrong. He turned away from the full-length mirror, and to his horror, discovered a hole on the back of the shirt.

Who was he kidding? This wasn't a hole. A hole is a minor inconvenience. There was more hole than shirt. This was a gap. A gap the size of a canned ham.

Taylor quickly dialed Steve's house, but got no answer. He could run to the store and buy a new shirt, but didn't have time.

"CRAP!" he yelled toward the mirror. Maybe no one would notice, he thought. Then, he scoffed at himself. That was like asking the Elephant Man to your prom and hoping nobody would notice. He had but one solution: a jacket. Taylor was planning to bring one anyway, but when it was 98 degrees nobody ever really put it on. He thought maybe he could discreetly turn up the air conditioner and make it a little cooler in the small bookstore.

Here it was, the biggest night of his career so far, with reviewers and television reporters coming, and all he could think about was turning up the air conditioner.

Grabbing the jacket, Taylor rushed toward his truck. The mini crisis had thrown him behind schedule. He would have to rush now. He put the key in the ignition and turned it. Nothing happened. Again, he turned the key. Nothing. He was on the verge of tears now. One more try. "Please God, please start this truck." Once again, nothing. Taylor looked back at Mrs. Floraman's apartment. She had already left. Another futile try at the ignition. The truck had finally died. He looked out the rearview mirror and saw the cross-town bus rumbling up San Pedro Avenue. He dashed from the truck, not even bothering to close the door. Like it mattered now.

Sprinting across San Pedro, he chased the bus for half a block before the driver stopped. Sweat poured off Taylor's forehead as he caught up to the vehicle's open door.

"Aren't you hot, wearing that coat and tie?" asked the driver.

"No, I prefer it this way," said Taylor as he fumbled for 75 cents. "Do you have change for a five?" The driver pointed to a sign above his head: *THE DRIVER DOES NOT MAKE CHANGE.* Taylor folded his last five dollars and crammed them into the fare box. This evening was starting off perfectly.

* * *

The bus slowed to a stop across the street from the Fig Tree. Arguably San Antonio's most dignified bookstore, it sat amidst the manicured streets of Alamo Heights, the blue blood section of town. The fact that this particular shop had asked to host the opening party was in itself gratifying to Taylor. His past openings were always at the Guenthers' cramped bookstore downtown. But this one was to be different. The only thing seeming out of place was the giant taco parked out in front of the store. Taylor had to laugh. Now, it actually just seemed right that it was there.

He crossed the street, slipped through the alley and then in the bookstore's back door. He ducked his head as he slid into the bathroom. The place felt like a furnace. While washing the dried sweat from his brow, he overheard a sales clerk on the phone. "What do you mean you can't come out tonight? We've got three hundred important people and no air conditioning!"

Taylor's eyes rolled. He was going to die tonight. He was going to melt into a puddle of his own perspiration. He finally was cleaned up and ready to meet the crowd. From the back of the bookstore he could see many friends and colleagues. He was more nervous than he been at the previous signing parties. Those were little more than an excuse for his friends to drink. But this one had drawn the attention of the public because it questioned the validity of the church's claim that Davy Crockett was buried in a tomb at the Cathedral. Reporters from all three stations and the local papers were there. *Texas Monthly* magazine sent a reviewer, which would immediately validate the work he had done. He looked for Logan, hoping that she would stand by his side and ease the discomfort of his temporary celebrity. Thinking about the crowd made him sweat again.

He spotted Steve in the corner talking to one of the prettier employees. "The Major has arrived!"

Taylor grabbed Steve by the arm and pulled him away from the girl. "Did you notice anything unusual about the shirt you gave me?"

"Let me see, white, starched, smells like the Salvation Army. No, I would say that is your run-of-the-mill Thrift Shop shirt."

Taylor pulled down his jacket. "Let me ask you this: don't most of these shirts have a back?"

Steve laughed when he saw the size of the hole. "I gotta show this to Joe; he'll get a kick out of it."

"Forget it, I'm nervous enough. I'm not going to become a laughingstock. Take your shirt off and give it to me. NOW."

Eric Bob Kaufman King found the pair in the corner and called to Taylor, "Where have you been? Everybody's been looking for you."

"My truck died and I had to take the bus."

Steve began to pull off Taylor's jacket, "Eric Bob, check out the size of this hole!"

"Jeez, that is the size of a ... "

"Canned ham," Taylor said, finishing his sentence. "Now, Steve, take off your shirt and trade with me."

"Just leave your jacket on," Steve complained.

"It will have to do for now," Eric Bob said as he pulled him toward the center of party. "I have implicit instructions from Kirk Dooley to bring you to him as soon as you get here. He is having a conniption."

Eric Bob dragged Taylor through the party, not letting him stop to say hello to any of the guests until he found the publisher, entertaining a circle of people. Eric Bob shoved the reluctant author into the group. "Taylor Nichols, where have you been hiding?"

Taylor leaned over to whisper into Kirk's ear and told him about his truck dying. Kirk, making the best of the situation, introduced him to the people around him, who included two editors from the publishing company and their spouses and a reporter from *Texas Monthly*.

"I'm Ellen Mallory from *Texas Monthly*," said a well-dressed, attractive woman in her 40s. "I got to read an advance copy of your book, and I was very impressed with your research. Have you heard any repercussions from the Catholic Church?"

Taylor was about to answer when the publisher cut in.

"Did we ever? It was a little touch-and-go there for a while. We were quite worried they would try to ban it.

But, I put on the old silk glove and smoothed things over for my boy."

"We?" wondered Taylor to himself. "You can only suppress the truth for so long, Ms. Mallory," the author said aloud. "I just happened to be the one who stumbled upon it."

"My boy is just being modest. His research is so thorough it makes the rest of my writers look like goddamn sixth graders." Kirk let out a hearty laugh and slapped Taylor on the back, feeling the shirt's hole through the jacket. Kirk quickly dropped his hand. He leaned into Taylor's ear. "You got that shirt from Steve, didn't you?"

"Any ideas for your next book, Mr. Nichols?" came a question from one of the spouses who sensed an embarrassing situation and was hoping to defuse it.

"As a matter of fact, I've already begun the research on my next book. It's about the city's relationship with water, the ancient acequias, the old Spanish aqueduct, the River Walk, the aquifer—"

"Sounds quite ... interesting," came a polite reply. Kirk's eyes rolled. It was obvious to him that the book would be a flop. Nobody reads about water. Maybe he should be happy that this Alamo book had such a successful launch. Three TV stations had come, the newspapers, *Texas Monthly*. He had been besieged by requests for advance copies. He declined all but *Texas Monthly*. The last thing he wanted was some cheesy TV news program to steal their thunder and expose the story before the book came out. Still, some went to terrific lengths to try to get an advance copy of the book. One person claimed to be sick in a nursing home in California and said he might not live to see it published. The bishop himself tried for months to get his hands on it. He had to wait, too. They all had to wait.

Taylor excused himself from the group, but not before Kirk asked him if the rewrites for *Urban Renewal* were ready. In his rush to get here on time, he had forgotten them at home. He had spent a major portion of the last two nights scanning the original manuscript, updating it for the next printing. He would have to bring the completed file to Kirk's hotel room tomorrow morning before he left.

The young writer wandered around the party, greeting guests, signing books and looking for the face of a friend, any friend. It seemed he did not even know most of the attendees. He took a few minutes to tape interviews with a couple of local TV stations and a news crew from Dallas. No matter how many reporters talked to him, though, they all asked the same questions.

"Your book reveals that the Davy Crockett tomb in San Fernando Cathedral is not the actual resting place of Davy Crockett. How did you discover this?"

"What reaction did the Catholic Church have toward your book?"

"Where do you think Davy Crockett was really buried?"

Feeling overwhelmed by the throng of people, Taylor stepped outside to grab some fresh air and came across Father Patrick walking up the steps. Dressed all in black, Taylor thought the priest must feel even hotter than him.

"Taylor Nichols, why are you not inside enjoying your party?"

"I just needed a break from all the 'meetin' and greetin.'' So many people are there that no one will miss me."

"You would make a lousy politician, my son."

"I've been here for an hour, and I haven't even seen my date."

"So, you decided to come outside. This is a good place to look for her, somewhere where nobody is."

Taylor looked toward the ground and chuckled. "I found you."

"Yes, this is true. And I am glad you did. Have you found out anything about St. Anthony's Retreat?"

"No, I haven't. But interestingly, the more I don't find out, the more I do."

"Please explain."

"Well, Father, it's like this. Everywhere I've looked I have found a dead end. I've searched the county archives, the Alamo Library, and the state archives and have found nothing. But on every step of the way, I've discovered that Father Olivares and Noel Black have already beaten me to the punch. It seems like those two are both searching for the same set of plans. Both seem to want them real bad, but I can't figure out why."

"Has Father Olivares checked up on you? As I recall, you left him the impression that you might have a set of blueprints."

"Has he checked up on me? He calls my house every hour! He has stopped by three times, according to my landlady. So far I've been lucky enough to keep missing him. I would like to know what exactly I'm looking for before I tell him I can't find it."

Father Patrick looked off across the street at nothing in particular.

"Father, you know what I'm looking for, don't you?"

"Taylor, I did a little checking. I know that the diocese is in need of money to sponsor the pope's visit to San Antonio. I believe that is why the retreat was sold. Outside of that, all I know is hearsay and speculation."

"How about sharing some of those rumors with me?"

"To do that now would jeopardize much. For now I must keep silent. But I do think it would be best to keep Father Olivares at arm's length. Especially if you find out anything." The priest winked at Taylor and wiped the sweat from his forehead. "It sure is stifling out here; I think I'll go inside and enjoy the air conditioning. You look hot yourself. Why don't you take off your jacket?"

As the priest walked into the bookstore, he was met by Karl Guenther and his nephews. The trio exchanged pleasantries before exiting into the hot evening air.

"Mr. Taylor Nichols, why are youz out here and not enjoying your party?

"Karl, I needed a little break."

"Why yes, you do. I saw your Logan friend inside. She is quite beautiful. You no let her go. You need a nice young lady friend. You spend too much time atop my building alone."

Ted and Ed rolled their eyes at their uncle's sermon. After telling Taylor that Logan was inside, they turned and reentered themselves.

"I am glad that my nephews have left. I must humbly ask for your help."

"Karl, anything for you."

"Well, Mr. Taylor Nichols," the old German spat out as it became apparent that he had indulged in too much beer, "as you probably know, I have decided to sell the ranch that my family has owned since before I was born. My brother is very upset about this, but I am old and the land has become too much of a burden for me."

Taylor nodded and wondered where this was leading. For the first time tonight, he began wishing he was inside.

"You know, I thought that one day I would sell to the Disney Company, but I was approached by a nice Polish man from one of the oldest Polish families in South Texas. They are originally from Panna Maria. At first I told him there was no way I would ever sell, but the more I thought about it, the more I thought it would be nice to live in town and not have to drive 30 miles every day to work and to church." Taylor knew that this was only a story; Karl wanted nothing more than to rid himself of the ranch. "This man, I have his name written down ... " The old man fumbled for his wallet, which was overflowing with pictures and such. "It is somewhere in here ... I put it here yesterday."

Taylor could already feel the request about to be made.

"Here it is," said the old German as he brought forth a scrap piece of paper with some scribbling on it. "Pietr Tzynczynski. Look at that name." He handed the paper to Taylor.

"This is the guy who wants to buy your ranch? What does he do? For a living, that is?"

"I'z don't know. I think he is retired, an older guy, said he grew up near here and wanted to retire in the country. I would like you to find out a little about his family if you could."

There it was. Find out a little about his family. What was he, a private eye all of sudden? The old German looked at Taylor as if he was owed for all the years he had let the young man sneak into the Tower Life Building late at night and trespass to the observation deck. Taylor knew the look and felt the obligation. He sometimes took for granted the special privilege afforded him. After all, the place had been closed for over twenty years.

"If you were able to find out about his family, if he was from one of the oldest Polish families in Texas, than maybe my brother would feel better about selling the property."

Taylor looked at the name, "Shouldn't be that hard; there can't be that many Tzynczynskis in the world."

"Exactly, that is what he said. They are the only family in the United States with that surname. He says he is the only living person with the name Pietr Tzynczynski. Named after his grandfather. Can you imagine being the only person in the United States with your name?"

Taylor had never really thought about it. But at least this should not be a time-consuming project: a quick trip to the town of Panna Maria to check with the only church in town and go through their records should do the trick. Maybe go through the phone book and talk to some relatives, find out some interesting stories about the family, something to set the Guenther family at ease. It shouldn't be that difficult, except for the fact that he no longer owned a vehicle that worked. "Karl, I would be pleased to help you out. Is there any way I can contact this Pietr Tzynczynski fellow?"

"Oh, sure, he gave me his card." Once again the old German began to search his wallet. This would have been a difficult task enough in a wallet like his, stuffed with old Army I.D.'s, union cards, and Knights of Columbus membership cards. But the search was taking twice as long because of Karl's near-intoxication.

"Karl, why don't I get that from you later?"

"Yes, I will look for it. I may have it at home. You know, Taylor, I am lucky that I got the opportunity to sell my land. It sits right on top on the aquifer."

Here went the story again. He had heard it a thousand times, from every rancher who ever wanted to sell land north of San Antonio. They all complained about sitting on top of the Edwards Aquifer recharge zone. Because they lived in an environmentally sensitive area, the property was zoned only for light farming or ranching. Even though the city was fast approaching them, their land would never fetch top dollar from developers.

" ... So, basically the land is of little value to anybody," Karl continued. "Unless you are like dis Pietr Tzynczynski, who just wants to retire. But you have heard all this before. Besides, it is late, I have had too much to drink, and I want nothing more than to get out of the heat, go to work and take a nap." The security guard hugged Taylor and strode off to catch a bus toward downtown. The author stuffed the name into his own wallet and was turning to go back into his party when he heard a car horn.

Pulling up in front of the bookstore was the Eyewitness News van. He immediately got a wave from the station's Russell Rhodes. "Taylor, glad I caught you."

"I can't believe it," he said. "I thought I would never see the day that the great Russell Rhodes was scooped by Channel 4 and Channel 12. The public station even got here before you."

"Yes, but did they go to the Alamo and interview the curator? NOOO. Did they go to San Fernando and interview the Monsignor in front of the supposed tomb of Davy Crockett? NOOO. Did they go over to the diocese office and interview the bishop's right hand man? NOOO. Are they going to have their stories air tomorrow night on the *CBS Evening News*? NO!" gloated the reporter.

"You're going to have your story picked up by the network!"

"Well ... no. But it could happen," Russell said. "This is big. You've really ruffled some feathers. The guy at the diocese is really pissed at you."

"His name wouldn't happen to be Father Olivares, would it?"

"That's the one. He didn't say anything bad about you. Kept it real cool for the camera, but I could tell there was something going on. Major, that's not a man to mess with. He's got the bishop's ear. He's the guy planning the pope's visit to Texas. He's not the guy to have mad at you. What's up with that?"

Russell Rhodes, always the inquisitor. Always wanting to know the real story. But still, one of the few reporters that Taylor trusted with the truth. He always got a fair shot with Russell. The two sat in front of the bookstore while the cameraman set up his equipment. Taylor told him about the meeting with Olivares on Monday and all that had happened since. He described how Olivares had been hounding him for those plans ever since he left the diocese office. "I really wish I could find them, but I am beginning to lose hope. I just wish I knew why everybody wanted them so bad."

"I don't know that, but I do know that the retreat was sold because the diocese needed money for the pope's visit. From what I understand, the bishop was not too pleased when he found out that the old place had been sold," the reporter answered.

"I don't know what's up, but they seem more interested in that old retreat than they are in my book. I thought they were going to go ballistic, but Father Olivares barely brought it up in our meeting."

The cameraman turned on his light and handed Russell his mic. "Well, the public could care less about the St. Anthony Retreat; they want to know about the man who exposed one of the city's most popular tourist attractions as a fraud. Can I ask you a few questions?"

"Sure, as long as you don't try to sensationalize it, you tabloid sleazoid," Taylor said in jest. He never questioned the reporter's fairness and always made sure he gave Russell more than just the standard 'press release' quotes. The pair bantered for a few minutes in front of the camera with the tape rolling. Taylor knew that this reporter always went the extra mile for his story. He obviously had spent some time on it already.

Later, as the camera lights went down, Russell changed his tone from conversational to hushed. "Hey,

I'm sorry about the story that ran Saturday morning on the Finck Building. It made you look bad. That was not my call. The producer clipped my story in the editing room. I was fuming. I went to my boss, but I could tell that someone else had made a call. I was heavily edited."

"I didn't think too much about it. I figured someone had spliced it up. They showed mostly footage and almost cut you out completely. But, there is one thing I don't understand. Why were you there at midnight on Friday night? Why did you even bother? Not that I mind, but why did I deserve to have the city's top reporter covering our little protest?"

"Taylor, let me tell you something. I'm a good reporter. But you need more than that these days to get noticed by the networks. You need the big story—like Dan Rather. He was just a young beat man in Houston when a hurricane hit, and his face was splashed all over the country. Next thing you know he's a network star. You've got to have that big story to get the network to notice you.

"I have this sixth sense, call it a reporter's instinct. You are going to lead me to that story. I don't know when, I don't know how, but I have this gut feeling that you guys are going to do something big one day, and I'll be there with my camera."

Taylor looked down at his own feet, embarrassed by the flattering words. "That's really nice of you to say."

"Yeah, I figure that one day you guys will crack and be on top of the Alamo with rifles shooting at tourists." Russell punched Taylor in the arm, winked at him, then got back in the van and waved goodbye.

* * *

The heat inside the bookstore was becoming unbearable. Despite that, the crowd had grown much larger than Taylor had expected. Who were all these people? Social mingling was never one of his strong suits. He finally found Logan and spent a half hour with her. She just floated through the crowd, chatting with Kirk and the woman from *Texas Monthly* as if they were the oldest of friends. When she was at his side—

actually, when he was at her side—he felt invincible. But for the most part, Taylor spent his time signing books at the front and hanging in back with Steve and Eric Bob, watching them scope out the pretty girls and make fun of the Alamo Heights crowd. He would rather have stayed with Logan, but he also felt an obligation to his friends.

"Check this out! I can hardly believe my eyes," said Eric Bob in a hushed tone.

"Is it that girl in the tight sweater putting books back on a top shelf," Steve mocked. "If it is, I've already seen that and it ... " Steve stopped, grabbed Taylor's arm and pointed toward the front of the store. Standing in line to purchase three copies of his book was Noel Black.

All three of them made a rush for the table until Taylor held up his arm. This was his party and his confrontation. He was going to handle it his way.

"Mr. Black, I never knew you were so interested in San Antonio's history," he said casually to the man in line.

Black looked up from the table not at all surprised. "Taylor Nichols, you know I have always been a fan of yours."

"Three copies?"

"I've always thought that it was my duty to be a patron of the literary arts, though to call your writing art is stretching it a bit, wouldn't you agree?" Black reached into his pocket and gave the cashier a credit card. By this time, Joe and Ella had slipped up behind Taylor to observe up close. Steve and Eric Bob had found the Gunther brothers and they continued to keep their distance.

As soon as the clerk ran the credit card across the purchase slip, Taylor reached down and tore it in half. Slipping the paper into his shirt pocket, he announced, "These are on me."

Black smiled, took the books without saying a word, and gave him a nod, then turned and exited the store. As he walked down the steps to his limo that was double parked behind the giant taco, a police officer was placing a ticket on his windshield. In the officer's pocket was a Travis Club cigar.

The whole scene was witnessed by the group that could not help but laugh. 'A perfect end to a perfect evening,' thought Taylor, forgetting about the less-than-memorable start.

"Who's going to pay for these books?"

Taylor turned to the salesclerk, who could care less about the silent battle that had just been waged.

"Somebody owes me $44.85 plus tax."

Remembering that he spent his last five dollars on the bus, Taylor glanced at Joe, who once again was prepared to open his wallet.

Chapter 13

Logan's car pulled into the glow of a familiar street lamp. Taylor was about to speak when she put a finger to her lips. She got out of the car and opened the trunk to reveal a picnic basket. Once again, she motioned for Taylor to be silent as she led him across the street and into the lobby of the sleeping building. Karl was there waiting, and held the elevator for the pair. The old German winked and smiled deviously as the elevator door slipped quietly shut.

Logan's manicured nails pressed the button for the 31st floor as she turned to Taylor and smiled. He knew now to be silent. When the elevator opened, she leaned toward him and whispered, "Take me to the top."

He gently took her hand while feeling his own fingers tremble. A hint of her perfume drew him further under her spell. He barely remembered how they had gotten to the Tower Life Building. The party had been winding down when Logan appeared at his side. He apologized for not spending more time with her.

"This was a big night for you," she had replied. "A lot of people came here to meet you. I understand."

Taylor practically floated up the steps, through the bathroom, over the toilet, and out the window, pulling her gently along. For the first time, he barely noticed the view from atop the observation deck. Instead, he noticed everything about her: the button she had undone on her blouse, the hair falling softly over her ear, and the delicate curve of her neck. For a rare moment he no longer felt like an awkward boy. She placed a finger under his chin, pulled him closer, and kissed him passionately.

"I'm so proud of you," she said, when their lips finally parted. She gazed deep into his soul and kissed him again. Slowly, she pushed the jacket from his shoulders until it fell to the concrete. Her hands moved across his back until she felt bare skin.

"You have a giant hole in your shirt," she said with a laugh, breaking the romantic moment.

"Why do you think I've been wearing this jacket all night long?" Taylor said sheepishly. "Steve loaned me one of his Salvation Army specials and I didn't realize until I put it on that this shirt had a hole."

"Hole? There's more hole than shirt!"

"You know, the back of the shirt is so overrated anyway. I like to think of myself as a trendsetter. Next year, all the guys in New York will be wearing their shirts like this."

Logan tried to suppress her laughter, sensing that he felt more embarrassed than he let on. She stepped away from their embrace and opened the picnic basket. Inside were two glasses and a bottle of champagne. "I wanted to celebrate your new book in a special way. Would you do the honors?"

Taylor popped the cork and filled the glasses, handing one to her. She leaned over the balcony, looking out toward the city as he embraced her from behind. She could feel his warm breath on the back of her neck. "Taylor Nichols, you are one in a million. Did you know that?"

"Did you know that with five billion people on this planet that means that there are 5,000 other people just like me?" he said, catching her off guard.

"You're such a brat! Can't you even take a compliment?" They both looked out to the horizon together. "Taylor Nichols, the great Taylor Nichols ... or should I call you Major Taylor?"

"Major Taylor? Why would you call me that?"

"You tell me. I notice that your friends often refer to you as 'the Major.' Plus, the other day I was looking back over your loan application when I noticed that your middle name was Taylor and your first name was Major. The cat is out of the bag. Now it's time to explain."

"My real name is Major Taylor Nichols."

"And? I need more of an explanation than that."

"That's my name, Major Taylor, but I've always gone by the name Taylor. What more do you need to know?"

"Well, I don't know. I've just never heard of anybody whose first name was Major. I just figured there had to be some reason behind it."

"When I was twelve years old, I asked my father why my first name was Major. He told me that Major Taylor was a great man that he very much admired, but history had all but forgotten about him. I asked what made him so great, and my dad told me that it was up to me to find out. I spent two weeks of my summer vacation in the library trying to find out who Major Taylor was. He was right when he said that history had forgotten him. But by the time I learned who he was, I also learned who I was. I realized why my father had named me after him, and why he made me find out for myself who he was. In a way I feel as if my father gave me a rare gift."

"So who was Major Taylor?"

"That's something you'll have to find out for yourself."

"Just tell me, Major Taylor."

"I could just tell you, but then I would have to kill you," he joked.

"I'm so curious! Go ahead tell me, then kill me." She stared into his eyes and waited for an answer. "You're really not going to tell me, are you?"

"No, I'm not."

"Do all your friends know?"

"Yes, they do."

"Did they all go look it up?"

"Yes, they did. But they're older than I was; it didn't take them two weeks to find out."

"I'll just ask one of them," Logan said.

"They won't tell you." He smiled, thoroughly enjoying the moment.

"I guess I'll just have to go to the library," she said, sulking.

"I'll help you out a little. Don't waste your time looking for a military hero."

Logan pouted and turned back toward the view. Taylor sensed that the romantic tide had changed.

"Have you thought any more about the job offer?"

"Yes, I have. I have decided not to take it," he confessed.

"What? You can't be serious!"

"I'm very serious. I've thought about it and it's not for me." Logan's displeasure shocked Taylor. He expected her to be disappointed, but she seemed almost angry.

"Let me ask you this, Major Taylor," she said, "What do you want from life?"

"What do I want from life?" He was confused by the question. "What do you want from life?"

Logan turned to him and gathered her composure. "What does any person want from life? I want a good job, a nice place to live. I would like a nice car. I want to sample some of the finer things that this world has to offer. These are not such unusual things to want. What is it that *you* want?"

"What do I want? To tell you the truth, Logan, I have never really thought much about it. I don't sit around at night thinking it would be nice to have a big fancy car. Sure, it would be nice to have a truck that worked. But that isn't my goal in life. My goals are different. I don't plan what I can get; I plan what I can give. Want and give, you see the difference? I want to write great books. I want to discover lost history. I want my words to inspire and enlighten. Perhaps my efforts so far have been minimal, but it's a start. When I turn 30 I don't want to look back at my short life and say that I own a great car and I visited some fantastic night clubs."

"Oh, excuse me. I guess the nobility of your poverty escaped me. Seems like you and your slacker friends have much more righteous goals." As soon as the word 'slacker' had left her lips, Logan regretted it. She saw immediately how she had offended him.

"Listen," Taylor said softly, staring at the ground. "I know that my friends and I do not live a very lavish lifestyle. But we are not poor because we find 'nobility in our poverty' or because we suffer some sort of 'liberal guilt.' We are poor because we are doing exactly what we want to do, and it just doesn't pay very well. Sure, I would like to have enough money so I wouldn't have to worry every month if I could make my rent. And I hope someday that I do. But I don't want to sacrifice who I am and what I want to accomplish just so I can supply myself with material wealth. That's why I would rather not take the job. It's not me. It's not what I want to do."

He looked up from the floor of the observation deck and into her eyes. She leaned over and kissed him on the cheek. She turned back toward the skyline as a tear began to fall down her cheek.

"It's late," she said, after a few more minutes slipped by. "I've got to go to Houston tomorrow on business. I was hoping to take our new director of community relations with me, but I guess it just isn't to be."

She packed the empty glasses into the picnic basket, but left the champagne bottle. As she was crawling back into the window, Taylor said jokingly, "I didn't know the job included a road trip."

PART II

Chapter 14

Logan's car slowed to a stop in front of Taylor's home. She leaned over and kissed him on the cheek, letting the engine run. "I've got to get going. I've got to leave for Houston in the morning."

"I was going to ask you upstairs."

"Perhaps another night, Taylor; I've got a long day tomorrow."

The author scrambled from the car and walked toward his back door while his date sped away. As he climbed the back stairs, he noticed Mr. Tibbs outside the door, patrolling back and forth and protecting his domain. He had few chances to mark his outer territory and was taking full advantage of it.

"How did you get out?"

Taylor discovered his answer when he noticed the back door wide open and his keys dangling from the lock. He suddenly remembered leaving them in the truck.

"Hello, anybody here?" He walked into the kitchen, expecting to find the gang drinking beers and taking liberties in his apartment. As he turned the corner into the living room, though, quite a different scene met him.

The place had been trashed. Books were torn up and thrown off the shelves. His file cabinets stood empty, with the contents scattered. Cushions from the couch lay strewn across the floor and the closets were ransacked. The bedroom looked no better. His clothes sat in a heap beneath overturned drawers. It wasn't until he had surveyed both rooms that he discovered his computer missing.

Taylor mentally inventoried his desk and discovered dozens of other missing items. All his computer discs had disappeared. So had many paper files. Only then did he rush to the bedroom and enter the walk-in closet. Looking up, he saw that the door to the attic had been moved. He pulled a chair over, lifted the panel and pushed his head through the opening. Turning on the closet lamp, he tried to deflect some light into the musty attic. His heart sank.

Every one of the Randall Hugley drawings was gone. Every blueprint, every sketch, every scrap of paper that had been carefully preserved and resting there for 50 years had vanished.

"How could I be so stupid?" Taylor cried aloud. He had known he was being followed, but with all the excitement of the last few days it had slipped his mind. He should have taken some precautions.

Should he have locked all his files in a safety deposit box? Should he have collected all his Hugley drawings and moved them to Joe's house? He really never thought he had anything that anybody would really want. But apparently others thought he did. He had been playing cat and mouse with Father Olivares for days now, making him think that he had the blueprints to the St. Anthony Retreat.

That was it, he thought. The good father had finally had enough of his evasive tactics. He was going to get what he wanted whether Taylor cooperated or not. Who else would be so interested in his files, his discs, and his drawings? It was Olivares who had a man following him. And leaving his keys in the truck, Taylor couldn't have made it easier.

He was about to call the police and report the break-in when he set the receiver back on its cradle. He picked up the phone again to call Joe, realizing he should have a lawyer present. "We'll demand a search warrant and get the good priest out of bed!" His heart raced and his thoughts came in a rush. "What am I thinking? A search warrant for Father Olivares!" What did he think, that the priest was that dumb? That he would just have all his stuff sitting in his office? Or perhaps it was spread out over the altar in the bishop's private chapel. He scoffed at himself as he dialed Joe's number.

Before he heard a ring, he set the receiver down a second time. A name popped into his head that he had totally forgotten about: Noel Black.

Noel Black could have broken into his house. Maybe not Black personally, but someone he had sent over to find what he was looking for. Black wanted those drawings just as badly as Olivares did. Everywhere he had searched, he had been preceded by both of them. Fear suddenly overcame Taylor as he became aware of how high the stakes were to these parties. They were so desperate to get their hands on the plans that they were willing to do almost anything. How far would they go?

His hands trembled as he dialed the police. How long ago had they left? If he had not gone to the rooftop with Logan, would he have run into them? Was he being watched now?

"San Antonio Police."

"Hello, I'd like to report a break-in."

* * *

It was 3:00 a.m. before the police arrived. They surveyed the damage, took a statement, and made a vain search for clues before leaving. The lack of a single fingerprint made it painfully obvious that this had been a professional job. The police surmised that the back door was left open because whoever had broken in was still there when Taylor was dropped off, and hearing him, had quickly fled. An officer had said there was little they could do because much of what was stolen was paperwork and computer files that really were not of any value. They asked if he knew of anybody who would want to break in and steal a bunch of papers. Because it was in the middle of the night and he did not feel like explaining to a third shift cop why he suspected either the bishop's right-hand man or the city's richest developer, he just mumbled a halfhearted, "I don't know."

It was 4:30 before he finally went to sleep. He didn't bother to pick up anything. He had all weekend to do that.

* * *

The phone rang at 9:00 a.m. and again at 9:01 and 9:02. Each time the caller would hang up before the answering machine picked up.

The fourth time, Taylor rolled over and grabbed the receiver. "Hello?"

"Taylor, this is Kirk. Kirk Dooley, you remember me, don't you? Your publisher. You know, the guy who sends you a royalty check every now and then. I was wondering if before I left town I could get those rewrites you promised me."

Rewrites. That was the last thing on his mind. Taylor's cloudy mind snapped back to reality as his eyes absorbed the mess from the night before.

"They're gone," he mumbled.

"Gone? What do you mean they're gone?"

"Gone," Taylor repeated as he slumped down onto his desk chair in his pajamas. "Gone, as in stolen."

"Jesus Christ, my plane leaves in an hour! I don't have time for games." Taylor wished it were all a game, a game he could stop playing.

Taylor spent the next 10 minutes explaining his past week to Kirk, including the climax upon his arrival home the night before. He had not realized it until this morning, but the rewrites for *Urban Renewal* were among the computer discs stolen the night before.

"Are you okay?" Kirk asked quietly.

"I'm fine, but everything I've ever worked on, every piece I've ever written, was taken last night, not to mention all the Hugley drawings. Who was I to keep those to myself? They should have been donated to a museum. Now they're gone too."

"All is not lost. I've got copies of all your work at my offices, with the exception of the rewrites and…. your 'Water' book. So, all that's really missing are your most current pieces. It's not a total loss."

"I guess it's not, if you don't consider the fact that my computer has been stolen too and I have nothing to even write on."

Kirk, realizing that Taylor was a bit more shaken than he would admit, offered a brotherly shoulder to lean on. "Don't worry, Taylor; I'm not going to let my most prolific author be without the tools to write. We'll get you a computer. I'll claim it on my insurance or something. We'll find a solution. But, first things first. We need to redo those rewrites, ASAP. We've reserved the printer for Friday to run off the latest edition of

Urban Renewal. That means we have to typeset on Wednesday and Thursday. Meaning we have to have it done by Tuesday. Can you come up to Dallas for a few days and work out of our office?"

A trip to Dallas was the last thing Taylor wanted. If ever a metropolis did not agree with him, it was Dallas. It was everything in a city he hated: loud, gaudy and pretentious. But he knew he had no choice. His back was up against the wall and he had an obligation to fulfill. "I'll leave Saturday after the radio show. That will give me Sunday, Monday and Tuesday. It shouldn't take more than two days if I work straight through."

"That's my boy. Don't worry, everything is going to be okay. I'll make copies of everything you've given me and we'll find you a new computer. Give me a call on Saturday when you get to town."

Taylor said his goodbyes and put the phone down. 'Don't worry,' he thought. That's easy for Kirk to say. Here he was sitting in the middle of the rubble that used to be his apartment and all Kirk could say was 'Don't worry.'

Taylor got up, kicked a broken lampshade and collapsed back into bed.

* * *

"Steve ... how would you like to go to Dallas?" Taylor tried to sound excited on the phone, but it did not matter because nothing could mask his desperation. He needed to go to Dallas, but his truck was finished. Joe, Eric Bob, Ted and Ed all had jobs. He knew that they could not take him. Steve, who never seemed to have permanent employment, also had a brother in Dallas who sometimes could be counted on for free room and board.

"Why Dallas?"

Taylor explained to him his dire straits. He needed to get the rewrites done by Tuesday night.

Steve thought to himself for a moment. "A trip to Dallas might not be such a bad idea. I could see if the taco car is a big hit there. Maybe it will take off and I could build a fleet of taco cars coast to coast. Major, it looks like we're going on a road trip!"

* * *

Friday night confession at St. Agnes was usually the slowest night of the week. Father Patrick once told Taylor that Saturday was the day to hear confessions. People wanted to unburden their souls before Sunday mass. Confessing sin was the last thing on his parishioners' minds on Friday.

"Bless me, Father, for I have sinned. I have not been to confession since the Cubs won the World Series."

"I hope you have had a better decade than the Cubs. What brings you to St. Agnes, Taylor? I know it isn't a confession, though that wouldn't be a bad idea."

"I was broken into last night, cleaned out."

"Cleaned out? What exactly does that mean?"

"Last night someone came into my apartment and took my files, my computer, my notes, and every scrap of paper I had ever written on."

"It sounds like they were looking for something specific."

"Exactly. Whoever broke in wanted information on the St. Anthony Retreat. Here's the worst of it: they broke into my attic and stole all my ... the ... Hugley drawings."

The father sighed, leaning back in his chair. "I see."

"Father, I'm scared. People are following me. Now they're breaking into my home. The police say that I must have just missed them. Everybody thinks I know something. I don't know squat. I need some answers."

The sound of someone entering the other confessional broke Taylor's train of thought. "Pardon me." The Father slid the screen shut. Taylor sat in silence, wondering how long had it been since he actually came to confess his sins and how he could have given up the traditions of the church so easily.

"Have I found another religion?" he asked himself.

Father Patrick reopened the partition and apologized for the interruption. "Duty calls. One must always be available to ease the suffering of his flock."

"Well, Father, it's time for you to ease my suffering. I need some answers. What am I mixed up in?"

"Yes, I suppose you do need some answers." The elderly priest settled in and leaned closer to the confessional screen. "Let me start way back when I was a young man. When I entered the priesthood, I felt I was destined for great things in the church. I graduated from the seminary and went to work as an assistant to Bishop O'Malley. At the time, the diocese in San Antonio was filled with priests from Ireland. In fact, the Bishop had grown up with my father, and they had immigrated here at the same time. I've always suspected that is why the Bishop took me under his wing. I was one of the few American-born Irish priests here.

"As I got older I became more of a confidante of the Bishop. Many felt that I was being groomed to someday take his place. But, I could also begin to see a change coming. At one time San Antonio had separate parishes for the Irish, Polish, German, Italian, and Alsatian settlers. Priests from Ireland were sent by the boatload to South Texas to preach to the immigrants. But eventually, the different cultures mixed into the melting pot and the local parishes were denationalized. In the meantime, immigrants from Mexico started to come to San Antonio and change the makeup of the diocese. Eventually the diocese became predominantly Hispanic and demanded a Hispanic bishop. Before long I knew that Bishop O'Malley would be the last in a long line of Irish bishops.

"Being so close to Bishop O'Malley, I learned that he had a special love for the St. Anthony Retreat. I still remember when it was built. The young Randall Hugley was brought in to design it. The Bishop loved to go out there alone. Very few of the church's leaders were ever allowed to visit. I myself have never visited it.

"When Bishop O'Malley died and Bishop Santiago took the reins of the church, I left the diocese office and took over St. Agnes. I knew that I was a relic; I was at the wrong place at the wrong time. My ambitions in the church were over.

"I still keep close contact with many people up at the office, though. I have learned that Bishop Santiago has also grown quite fond of the retreat, often visiting alone like his predecessor. At the Bishop's right hand is young Father Olivares, a man who has designs on the bishop's ring and perhaps more.

"He is the one who has been organizing the pope's visit to San Antonio, an unprecedented event. Unfortunately, our diocese can barely afford the huge expense involved with a papal visit. Father Olivares, who has stuck his neck out and risked his career, needed to find funding fast. He decided to unload a piece of property that he thought the church no longer needed. He sold the St. Anthony Retreat at a price that guarantees that the papal visit budget will be met. Unfortunately, he did this behind the bishop's back."

Taylor, who had been spellbound by Father Patrick's monologue, began to shift uncomfortably. "So, Olivares gets himself in hot water for selling the retreat. I don't see where I'm involved."

"Very few people have ever visited the retreat. Some say there is a reason for that, that there is something holy about the place. That is, something sacred, which is why the bishops were drawn there. Now the church desperately wants it back. My guess is that Noel Black has figured that out and desperately wants to keep it to himself."

"What do you mean, something sacred, something holy? You're worrying me, Father."

"I don't mean to. But it has been said for years that Randall Hugley designed more than a building; he designed a conduit for the soul."

"A conduit for the soul? Father, what are you talking about?"

The father could hear the nervousness in Taylor's voice. "You, my son, are the foremost expert on the life and work of Randall Hugley. If you find the plans to the St. Anthony Retreat, you can find what is so special about this little place in the valley. Both Olivares and Black want to make sure they are the only ones who ever know."

Chapter 15

Taylor spent most of Friday night cleaning his apartment. Eric Bob Kaufman King came over after work and helped, as did Joe. Mrs. Floraman spent most of the afternoon going door-to-door, warning neighbors to be on the lookout for anything or anyone suspicious in the neighborhood. Though he appreciated the effort, Taylor felt it totally unnecessary. The assailants had already cleaned him out. They wouldn't be back.

At around eight Joe left for home and Eric Bob went out for some beer. They finished cleaning up an hour later and spent the rest of the evening sipping cans of Pearl and hoping for a cool breeze to hit the balcony. Though San Antonio was a dreadfully hot city, Taylor rarely used his air conditioner. The two antiquated wall units that Mrs. Floraman provided worked well enough, but they made his electric bill soar. It was a luxury he could not afford.

Electricity, rent, phone, and car insurance were his only expenses. And those were kept to a minimum. Mrs. Floraman paid the water bill, which was always incredibly cheap. The Edwards Aquifer provided an abundant water supply from which San Antonio drew freely. For so many years the city pumped as much free and clean water as it liked. San Antonio did not have a single reservoir or water treatment plant. It did not need one. The water, naturally filtered, was arguably the cleanest in the country. It seemed that only during the last few years had anybody become concerned with the level of the aquifer. Many felt that the city should build a reservoir as backup. Others believed that the supply was practically unlimited. The only thing for sure was that no one knew for sure.

For people like Taylor, all that mattered was having one less bill to pay. San Antonio was the perfect city for the Travis Club. One could get by with very little money in the Alamo City. Not only were expenses low, but so was entertainment.

No other city had as many festivals as this one. There was always an excuse to throw a street party that attracted the young and poor. San Antonio practically shut down in April for Fiesta. When the city drained the River Walk every February to repair its retaining walls, people came from around the country to celebrate the "Mud Festival."

The Guenther Brothers were working a fajita booth that night at another one of the city's seemingly endless series of festivals and had invited everyone down for cheap beer and free food. Normally Taylor would have joined the crowd, but tonight he didn't feel like celebrating.

Saturday morning, he headed to the neighborhood taco house like he did every week to enjoy breakfast with the Travis Club. The Guenther Brothers were already there and had taken the choice seats facing the Butter Krust Bread billboard with its mechanical loaf endlessly dumping slice after slice on the white plate with gingham trim. The rest of the club arrived shortly afterward, including Steve, who parked the taco car across the street so as not to raise the ire of the owner.

The talk of the morning was the robbery and the information Father Patrick had given Taylor. What was so special about the St. Anthony Retreat? The Guenther Brothers believed that there had been a vision of the Virgin Mary on one of the inside walls.

Eric Bob Kaufman King laughed at the suggestion. It was a typical reaction in a city that was nearly 60 percent Catholic. San Antonians were forever seeing the image of the Virgin Mary in a tortilla or on a reflection of a water tower.

Taylor bit into his tortilla without checking for the face of the Blessed Virgin and announced, "Whatever makes the St. Anthony Retreat so special will always remain a mystery to us. I never had the plans. I never will have the plans. And whoever broke into my apartment now knows this. It won't be long before they realize it and leave me alone."

"Maybe not," responded Joe, who was seemingly paying more attention to a pattern on his own tortilla. "All the people who broke into your place know is that you didn't have the plans there. They may deduce that you put them someplace else for safekeeping."

Taylor sighed, knowing that Joe made sense. Steve took a tortilla off Joe's plate and examined it for any religious irregularities, then loaded it with a healthy helping of pico de gallo. Just then, the cook came out and pinched his ear. "How many times have I told you not to park that taco car near my restaurant? It's bad for business. It advertises another restaurant."

"I parked it across the street," Steve protested.

"Next time, park it further down the block, so I can't see it." The cook then turned to Taylor and pointed sternly at him. "And you Mr. Big Shot on TV. Where is your girl this weekend? Did you lose her again, already?"

"She's gone to Houston to get some real Mexican food."

The cook laughed and tugged on Taylor's ear. "You get in that taco car with your friend and never come back." She turned her back to Taylor and vented her mock anger toward Joe. "José Reyes, you need to find a new group of friends!"

She walked back to the kitchen chuckling to herself. "Before you go, Taylor Nichols, come sign my book."

* * *

Taylor wished he had remembered to ask Eric Bob for a ride to the radio station. It was not until he got back home that he remembered that the truck was dead. He had not even bothered to open the hood to see if it was something simple that he could possibly fix. Deep down, though, Taylor knew that the truck had seen its last days. It barely passed its safety inspection last year and probably would not pass this year. Not being able to secure a loan, he would have to scrape up some cash and buy a cheap used car. It's amazing what you could get for $800. You just never knew how long an $800 car was going to last. But, that was a problem for another time. Right now he needed to hurry and catch a bus if he wanted to make it to the station before his show started.

He hated riding the bus. It reminded him of his days in college before he had a car. He had wasted countless hours waiting for transfers around the city. And here he was, once again on a bus, silently wishing for the day he could go to a big car dealership and pick out a new car—one with air conditioning—that would last for more than a year. One that would simply get him from point A to point B and would keep him from ever riding the bus again.

The first thing he noticed when he arrived at the station was the Mercedes parked out front. The station manager was here. Since Taylor came in only on Saturdays, he rarely saw the man. He stopped for a moment to remember to call him Mr. Gelman and not Jerry as he had done in the past. He did not like it when the air staff called him Jerry. Good rule to remember, just in case he ran into him in the hall.

"Where have you been?" Eric Bob whispered with panic. "I've been calling you for the last 20 minutes."

"Relax, I had to take the bus and it takes forever," Taylor said calmly. "What's the worry? We've still got 15 minutes until air time."

"Something's up. Something is going on. Gelman has been in the control room four times in the last half hour looking for you. He wants you in his ... "

"Taylor!"

Taylor had not even seen the station manager walk up behind him. "Can I see you for a moment in my office?"

Eric Bob looked away from the boss and into Taylor's eyes, passing along his concern. Taylor walked down the hall, feeling as if he was being sent to the principal's office. Only he did not know what for.

Gelman pointed to a chair as he shut the heavy door. "Take a seat." Taylor had rarely been in the inner sanctum except for a couple of times to discuss his contract. He always was amazed at how much nicer this office was compared to the rest of the station. With the cherry wood furniture and the plush carpet, it almost seemed as if he was in another building altogether.

"Radio is not like other businesses."

Taylor could already tell from the station manager's odd comment that he was not going to like the rest of this speech.

"You can have an employee who busts his butt for you every day, but he may not have what it takes to bring in the ratings to make his show successful.

You've been a great asset to the station, but unfortunately, the ratings just aren't there. I hope you understand. It's not that we don't appreciate the efforts that you've given us. We just feel that it's time for a change."

Taylor sat there, feeling a lump grow in the back of his throat. Ratings? Change? "Time for a change? Do you want me to make some changes in the show?" Taylor asked even though he knew that's not what he meant.

"Uhhhh, well, yes. I mean no. Taylor, we've decided to ... cancel your show. But, Taylor," Gelman said, raising his voice optimistically, "I don't want you to think that it has anything to do with you. We think you have done an excellent job. We just feel that your show is not what the listeners of this station want to hear." He turned away, not wanting to look in the young man's eyes. "I'm sorry, but we are going to have to let you go."

Taylor was taught not to burn his bridges. Hey, the show didn't work out. Well, no hard feelings. Let's shake hands and be grateful that we at least got a chance. That was the tack that he normally would have taken. But Gelman could not even look him in the eyes when he was firing him. Because they both knew ratings had nothing to do with this. They were not even in a ratings period.

Taylor could have just turned from the door and walked out, but he knew that it didn't really matter anyway. He got up, walked to the desk and leaned toward Gelman's face. "Who is 'we'?"

"Huh?"

"Who is 'we'? Who is this mysterious 'we' that has decided that I needed to be fired?"

"We ... uh, well that was decided, uh what I mean ... "

"What's going on here? I've never heard one negative thing from you people. Six months ago, you were begging me to extend my contract. You told me that you've just purchased three stations in Texas and that there is talk about taking the show statewide. And don't give me this ratings crap! You know what I replaced on this station? A show about cooking. What kind of ratings did that bring you?" Eric Bob had once told him that the cooking show received so few calls that the guy in the control room once fell asleep. "Tell me what's really going on here!" Taylor stood his ground.

"We've ... I've decided to make a change, that's all."

"This is wrong. You don't just fire a man out of the blue." Taylor leaned further into the face of Gelman. "Be a man, Jerry; tell me the truth. What's really going on here?"

The station manager rose from his chair and picked up the phone. "Mr. Nichols, our association has ended. I must ask you to vacate the premises or I will call building security."

Taylor turned raised his hands in defeat. "Okay, it's your radio station, you do what you want. All I asked is that you give me the real reason why I'm being let go." He shut the door gently behind him and walked toward the control room to tell Eric Bob the news. He could hear the top of the hour newscast over the station intercom reverberate throughout the halls.

"And as the chain of dry rainless days continues, the aquifer continues to drop. I'm Bob Guthrie, WOAI News. Stay tuned now for 'Cooking with Judy'."

Chapter 16

"Dallas is a woman that will walk on you when you are down."

Jimmie Dale Gilmore

The giant taco bounced into Taylor's driveway and Steve hit the horn. Immediately, a horde of neighborhood kids swarmed to the car. Taylor gave a wave out the window as he finished giving Eric Bob instructions over the phone on feeding Mr. Tibbs for the next few days. Then he grabbed his overnight bag, slid a key under the mat, and headed downstairs. On the way, Taylor stuck a note on Mrs. Floraman's door, letting her know he would be out of town. He wondered if he even needed to lock his doors after what had happened Thursday night.

Taylor threw his bag into the back seat and climbed in front as Steve started the giant taco and eased out of the driveway.

"You want some good news?" queried Steve, hoping to cheer up his passenger. "I called my brother and he said we could stay with him."

That was good news. Under any other circumstances, he would have rather stayed elsewhere. Steve's brother was always bragging, flashing his money or his latest purchase. It was hard to believe that he and Steve were related. But, Taylor was short on funds as it was and getting fired from the radio station certainly did not help. He could put up with him for a few days if it meant saving some bucks.

"More good news," said Steve, smiling.

"You're quite the angel of mercy today."

"You remember the Brownstone Company?"

"The company that bought The Finck Cigar Building," replied Taylor. "Yes, I remember."

"You have an appointment Monday afternoon with the President of the Brownstone Company."

"I do?" laughed Taylor. "How did you manage that?"

"Well, I figured that you needed a little cheering up. Eric Bob called me and I heard about you getting fired. So, I thought, 'what makes you happiest?' Then, it hit me. You're at your happiest when you are chained to a toilet or standing on one in order to climb out a window. Well there are no toilets that I know of in Dallas that need saving, so I did the next best thing. I called the president of Brownstone and told him that Taylor Nichols, the renowned writer from *Texas Monthly*, would like to do a story on their company and the saving of the Finck Building."

"I bet they jumped at the chance for some free publicity."

"Well, to be honest, they were very reluctant. I told them that the story was going to be with or without the interview, so they might as well participate."

"What did they say to that?"

"They finally agreed. But, then it made me think. We really don't know much about this Brownstone Company. So, as a good Travis Club member I did a little checking."

"And ... ? What did you find?"

"Very little. The company is not publicly owned, so there are no annual reports. I checked the vertical file.

Zilch. Did a search for magazine articles and once again, blank."

"What do you make of it?"

"I think I'm a lousy researcher. I tried, though; I really tried. We can't all be the great Major Taylor."

"Au contraire, I think you have found out a lot. We have a company that shuns publicity, even when it does public good. It is privately owned, so they don't have to open their books to anybody. There aren't any magazine or newspaper articles about them that we can find. Plus, it's a company that deals with Noel Black. It sounds as if the Brownstone Company may not be the savior that we were hoping for."

Steve smiled, realizing his efforts were not in vain. He had spent a lot of time in the library and had searched diligently, impressing a cute librarian he would be seeing later in the week.

The taco merged onto the freeway and chugged toward Dallas. As the car got further and further away from San Antonio, the reaction of motorists changed. Closer to the Alamo City, the car was viewed with awe.

You could almost hear the kids shriek as they spotted the famous auto. As they continued on the trek, the vehicle became an oddity. People laughed and Taylor thought he now knew how the shark boy at the carnival must feel. At one time, Steve had worn a hat shaped like an oversized jalapeño pepper. But, luckily Steve soon figured that driving an overgrown piece of food around town did not mean he hadn't any self-respect left.

Taylor knew that this was one road trip where he would get a chance to drift off to sleep. Steve rarely allowed anyone to drive the taco car. Taylor closed his eyes and tried to relive the past few days. It seemed like they had flown by, and once again his life was spinning out of control. It was just a week ago that he was in Logan's office begging her bank for a loan and walking out with a dinner invitation instead. Every moment since then, his life had been upside down.

"You're thinking about her, aren't you?" asked Steve.

"How did you know?"

"You've been grinding your teeth ever since you closed your eyes, and all of a sudden you started to smile. Are you falling for this woman?"

"She definitely is different from the others I've dated."

"You mean 'cause she's rich."

"She's not rich," Taylor protested. "She's successful. And I have no problem with that."

"I hope not. There aren't very many men who would pass up a ride in a European sedan with a gorgeous lady to ride to Dallas in a giant taco. But, I can tell you have some reservations. Is it the job?"

"No, I think she understands why I don't want it. You know, most people would look at us and say that I can't handle the relationship because she's so much more successful than I am. But it's not that at all. I love the fact that she is so confident and has done so well for herself."

"Then what is it?"

"It's kind of hard to explain. It's the way she looks at me. She gives me this look like I can do anything, like I'm some kind of Superman. It's almost as if she believes I'm perfect."

"And you hate that?"

"It's like this, Steve. There are two kinds of people who believe in you, those who think you can do anything because you are perfect, and those who know you only succeed because you're just so hard headed that you never give up. You, Joe and everybody else in the club know how many times I've failed at things and how many of my ideas didn't pan out. You know that I may not be the world's greatest writer, but I've succeeded because I've used persistence and hard work to make up for a lack of talent. She makes me feel the opposite ... and I feel like I'm living a lie."

"Taylor, you're a pathetic sap. You're worried that this girl thinks that you are too good? No wonder you never get laid."

Chapter 17

"Few cities in America provide as many startling contrasts as San Antonio. One realizes this quickly on their first trip to the Alamo, a monument whose stately presence is surrounded by a bustling downtown. When walking through downtown, visitors are startled to see such sights as the façade of a 1920s movie house decorating the ground floors of a corporate skyscraper, or an ancient downtown department store thoughtfully readapted into a modern urban shopping mall with a spectacular glass enclosed River Walk addition.

When it comes to urban renewal, San Antonio provides an excellent case study of two types of redevelopment, often across the street from each other. On one side of downtown, you have the failed Vista Verde Project, an example of the slum clearing policies that were popular with U.S. city planners in the 1960s and '70s. Across the street you have El Mercado, the old Mexican Market, which was successfully redeveloped by restoring the historic buildings.

On the east side of downtown, you find La Villita, the oldest part of the city that was rebuilt into a beautiful space for artisans and craftsmen but lacks foot traffic and often looks deserted. Across the street, you have Hemisfair Park, an old neighborhood that was cleared for the 1968 World's Fair, then, with the exception of the Convention Center sat vastly underused for 20 years. Once again, two contrasting styles of urban renewal, but this time with similar results.

This book will examine various cases of renewal and adaptation and the success and failures that followed. We will also examine various groups and their effect on shaping the city's future. Groups such as the Conservation Society who saved the San Antonio River from shortsighted city planners who wanted to pave it over and create parking lots. And the Catholic Church, which battled to retain control of the Alamo and lost, but still maintains active parishes in the remaining missions."

From the book *Urban Renewal in San Antonio*: *A History of Success and Failure* by Taylor Nichols - Third Edition

Taylor sat and stared at the computer screen, rereading the words he had written soon after college. He thought to himself of all the work he had put into updating the third edition and all the notes he had accumulated for naught. Now he would have to update the newest edition from memory. For the most part that would not be a difficult task, except for dates, which he could never hope to remember. But overall, the project would be extremely time consuming. Take, for instance, the chapter on Hemisfair Plaza and La Villita, two urban renewal projects across the street from each other. Since the last edition was printed, Hemisfair Plaza had built a water garden around its Observation Tower and had announced plans for a River Walk extension. Across the street, the old pathways of La Villita had nearly been turned into a "festival marketplace," but community pressure had insured that the little village would remain an oasis of peacefulness amidst the hustle of downtown.

From Taylor's standpoint, *Urban Renewal* had taken on a life of its own. Ever since the book was picked up as a textbook by numerous universities, he had felt he had lost control of it. The book constantly needed updating. It took a constant effort to catalog the number of projects in a city the size of San Antonio, especially in the last couple of years, when San Antonio really began to appreciate the older architecture that other Texas cities had torn down years before.

At the turn of the century, San Antonio was the biggest city in Texas. Houston, with its newly dredged ship channel, and Dallas with its railroads, began to surpass the Alamo City in the 1920s. But, San Antonio remained Texas' most exciting city, with the newly constructed Tower Life Building, known as the Empire State Building of the west, and the Milam Building, the world's first totally air-conditioned skyscraper, that was home to the state's most powerful oil and gas men. The city boasted world-class theaters like the Texas, the Majestic, and the Aztec. When the stock market crashed in 1929, however, the city of San Antonio never recovered. After the World War II, Dallas and Houston boomed, while San Antonio stagnated. Forty years later, the city looked virtually the same. It was the 1968 World's Fair that brought the city back to life. The first new hotel in four decades was built. The River Walk was extended and cleaned up. But, more important, the city finally woke up from its slumber.

Fortunately for the city, it had been comatose during the slash and burn urban renewal days of the early sixties. Ironically, the most destructive of these projects was Hemisfair Park, which tore down hundreds of homes, stores, and even churches, all in the name of progress. Unlike Dallas and Houston, the rest of downtown remained intact. Throughout the 1970s and 80s, the city became a boomtown. Hundreds of old buildings were restored and adapted for modern uses.

The old Lone Star Brewery became the Museum of Art. The Majestic Theater was renovated and hosted concerts and Broadway plays. The ancient Armory became a corporate headquarters. The old MoPac Train Depot was reborn as a credit union. The Medical Arts Building became the Emily Morgan Hotel. The Carnegie Library transformed into a Circus Museum. The list went on and on. San Antonio, with its old world charm, became a favorite destination of every Texan, as well as tourists from around the world.

Unfortunately, it also attracted developers such as Noel Black, who sought to exchange the city's charm for quick profits by tearing down historic properties and putting up a monument of glass and steel. Already gone were the Bluebonnet Hotel, the Chinese Elks Lodge, the Texas Theater, and many other treasures.

It was late Monday night, and Taylor sat alone in the darkness of his publisher's office, chronicling the success and failures of San Antonio's rebirth. He had been at it since arriving early Sunday morning via the taco car. Except for a few hours' sleep early Monday morning he had worked straight through the night.

Kirk found him sleeping on the floor of his office, the imprint of a fake oriental rug on his face, and woke him up telling him to go home. Taylor refused and continued writing. It was almost Tuesday, and the only clues to signify the passing of time were the squashed Coke cans and the empty Taco Bell bags in the trash can. Taylor had to laugh to himself when Kirk brought him a bag full of burritos from the fast food outlet. No self-respecting San Antonian would ever eat at Taco Bell.

At about 2:00 a.m. on Tuesday, Taylor finished and called Steve's brother's house. Exhausted but wired from the pressure, he and Steve finally found an all-night coffee shop and scarfed down someone's idea of a hamburger.

Steve, who dined on a soggy waffle, wanted to drive around a little longer afterward and look for an all-night Mexican restaurant, but this was Dallas, not San Antonio, where thousands of third-shift civil servants at Kelly Air Force Base kept restaurants open 24 hours.

"I didn't think you would finish so fast," said Steve, as he pushed his waffle around with his fork, quietly hoping that Taylor would pick up the tab and not deplete his already-low cash supply.

"It's easy to finish when you do a crappy job. All my notes are gone, so I had to write from memory. A lot of dates were left out; updated photos were missing. Definitely not my usual effort. But, I had to get it done quickly or we would miss the beginning of the fall semester and all the textbook sales. And, believe me, right now that is one thing I can't afford to miss." Taylor dug into his hamburger, wondering if he sounded as if he had sold out. "What have you been up to, besides being driven up the wall by your brother?"

"Let me see, I went to the sixth floor exhibit to see where Kennedy was shot, I went to the Galleria with my brother and watched him buy a pair of shoes that cost more than my rent, and I had to endure two days of lectures on how I am the ultimate slacker and could I please keep the taco car in the garage. So, all and all it's been a good trip."

"Steve, have you noticed that people in Dallas don't take to the taco car like they do in San Antonio?"

"I know. Any hope of franchising my creation died at the city limit sign." Steve pushed his waffle around in the syrup and took another disinterested bite.

Taylor stared through the window at the giant taco. "Do you ever wonder if we are doing the right thing?"

Steve picked up his fork with a skewered piece of waffle on the end of it and examined it closely "I know we're not. We should have looked harder for some Mexican food."

"No, I mean this whole Travis Club business. Do you ever wonder if what we are doing is right?"

"Of course what we're doing is right. Isn't it?"

"I don't know. I was updating my book, going over all the projects that have happened recently in San Antonio, and it's amazing how many things we've had our hands in. Like the Finck Building. Who are we to tell Noel Black what he can do and not do with his building? He bought it."

"Sure, he bought the building, but every city has certain zoning restrictions. You can't put a waste site next to your home; you can't build a liquor store next to a school. If you don't like the zoning ordinance, you can do two things: try to change the ordinance or move your business somewhere else. When we decide to live in a city, we have to make some compromises if we intend to live peacefully. I can't drive as fast as I want through downtown. I can't burn trash in my driveway. I can't build a 200-foot wall and block the sun from shining on the rest of the neighborhood. It's the same thing but on a larger scale. We, the people of San Antonio, have decided we want to preserve some of our architectural heritage. There are certain buildings we deem historic, an important part of our past. We, as a community, have passed laws to protect our heritage. If you buy a historic building, you know all this before you plop your money down. If you don't want to abide by our rules, fine. Either change them or take your money elsewhere and buy some other building. Buying a historic building and tearing it down to save on taxes is wrong. If all you want is a vacant lot, then buy one. Don't create one by tearing down the Finck Building."

Taylor looked stunned at Steve's thought process. "Wow, well put."

"Thanks, but I see what you mean. I always wonder if what we are doing is right."

* * *

The taco pulled into the parking lot of the Brownstone Company at promptly nine o'clock. Steve's desire to sleep in was exactly what Taylor had hoped for. He always had a secret desire to be mocked and ridiculed while driving a giant taco during rush hour. Besides, it was rare when Steve let anyone drive his creation, and he wanted to take advantage of this unusual opportunity.

He had no trouble finding the offices with the help of a map that Steve's brother had given him, but he was surprised by the area of town it was in. He expected to find an old house or building gracefully converted into offices. Instead, he found a soulless warehouse in the middle of a suburban light industrial park. The long one-story building had a tenant on either side of the Brownstone slot. To the left was a warehouse for a vending machine company, and to the right, the office of a Taco Bell franchisee.

Taylor parked the car around the corner facing the Taco Bell offices. A man inside gave him a disapproving smirk. Taylor looked down at the sidewalk and continued on.

Dressed in a white shirt he had borrowed that morning from Steve and a tie from his brother, he looked quite the part of a young reporter as he entered the office. "Excuse me," he said to a receptionist who was more interested in a magazine than greeting visitors. "I have an appointment to see Mr. Summerville."

"You mean Mr. Summerhill."

Taylor looked down at the small piece of paper where Steve had scribbled down the name of the company president. Summerhill, Summerville, it could have been either, what did it matter now? He had already made a fool of himself. "Ah, yes, that's right, Mr. Summerhill."

"And you are?" queried the receptionist, who acted as if she were doing him a big favor by picking up the phone to page Summerhill's secretary.

"Taylor Nichols. I'm writing a book about urban renewal and historic preservation. I have a nine o'clock appointment." Taylor sat quietly in the reception area. He glanced around at the artwork on the wall, expecting to find photographs of some of the other historic properties that the company had renovated. Instead he found a poster celebrating teamwork by depicting a men's rowing team. He waited for 15 minutes before a well-dressed woman in her forties came to the front and asked him to follow her. As he passed the receptionist's desk he could see the president's office at the end of the hallway. He made note of the other offices that were all situated off one main hallway. None of the workers looked anything at all like architects or designers. The offices were void of any of the tools that they might have. The walls in the hallway were decorated with more framed posters depicting generic workplace inspirations like *"Fortitude!"* The place looked more like an office for accountants than for people who restored historic buildings.

When the woman reached the end of the hallway, she politely knocked on the door and announced his arrival. "Mr. Summerhill, your nine o'clock is here." She ushered Taylor into a dimly lit workplace equipped with modern office furniture.

"Hi, I'm Taylor Nichols, the writer."

"Yes, of course, I'm Ed Summerhill. What is it we can do for you this morning?"

"I'm updating a book on urban renewal and historic preservation in San Antonio. This is used on many college campuses as a textbook. I was hoping to include a bit about the Finck Cigar factory. It's got an amazing history and the story is quite fascinating when you consider that the building was almost lost."

"Mr. Nichols, I'm a little confused, you say the building was almost lost?"

"We believe that the previous owner purchased the building with the intention of tearing it down. When he found that he would be unable to do so, he sold it to another party."

"You give me the impression that we purchased damaged goods, that we got taken in a fire sale. Let me assure you that we had been negotiating with the owner of the building for quite some time. There are a lot of problems with historic buildings: asbestos removal, updating fire escapes and sprinkler systems and bringing those up to code, not to mention adding central air conditioning and a modern phone system to a building that was built before those devices existed."

As every second ticked off the black numberless clock behind him, he could sense Summerhill's displeasure growing. Taylor's chair seemed to be sinking further and further below the desk.

"We offered Mr. Black, the owner, a price that may have seemed low to the layman like yourself, but, believe me, when you consider the cost of renovating a historic building, often it is more profitable just to tear it down and start over. Mr. Black could have done that, but he chose to take our offer and save the building. He took a loss, and we made an excellent buy. But, there is a long way to go before that building is usable again, not to mention profitable."

Summerhill's subtle insults did not go unnoticed by Taylor. He did not have to be reminded of the complexities of restoring historic buildings. He resented feeling like the boy who broke the neighbor's window, but he masked his emotions. He almost felt as if he were being provoked into a taking a 'go to hell, I'll write my book without you' stance.

"May I ask what your plans are for the building?"

"At the present, we have many different options for the Finck Building. Unfortunately, we are not prepared to discuss any. Mr. Nichols, I feel as if I may be wasting your time. You see, when you are in the business of restoring historic buildings such as we are, you must be careful not to offend local sensibilities. This is our first venture in San Antonio, and we are being very careful not to appear to be some robber baron who wants to make a killing gutting a local landmark while skirting taxes with an abatement. We like to keep a low profile. I tried to tell your assistant who made the appointment this, but he was quite insistent."

Summerhill looked at his watch, then at the door, as if to signify that Taylor should be leaving soon.

"Mr. Summerhill, I understand your point completely. I appreciate you letting me take a few moments from your busy schedule. As for my assistant, please accept my apologies. I asked him to set up an interview with you and not to take no for an answer." He got up from his chair, but paused as he was escorted to the door. "One quick question. I'm not very familiar with your company. What other buildings have you redeveloped?"

"Most of the properties we have worked with are in the Midwest, many around Chicago. I'm sure you have never heard of them."

"I'm sure I haven't. Thank you again for your time. I can find my way out." Taylor stepped out of the office and closed the door behind him. He wanted nothing more than to get out of there as soon as possible. He motioned to the secretary that he could find his way back, and started walking down the long hallway toward the front door. He hung his head low and walked slowly in a defeated gait. If the man in a side office had not sneezed and had Taylor not lifted his eyes to say 'Bless you,' he would have missed it.

On the door was the name Pietr Tzynczynski.

The polish spelling of the name Peter. The last name void of all but one common vowel. This was not your everyday name. There were very few people with a name like that. Perhaps, only one. He opened his wallet and found the scribbling that Karl Guenther had given him at his signing party.

"Excuse me, are you Mr. Zin-Chen-ski?"

"Why, yes I am, Zin-sin-ski. Pardon my name. It's kind of intimidating."

"I'm sorry, Mr. Zin-sin-ski. I believe we have a mutual acquaintance."

Chapter 18

The taco car sputtered loudly into the driveway, but even though it was 11 p.m., the rumble did not wake Steve. Not having steady employment, he rarely concerned himself with waking up early. Besides, he had spent most of the night catching up on movies on cable. Taylor burst into the house and found his compadre stretched out on the couch.

"Dogpile!" Taylor screamed, launching himself and plopping onto the couch. "Wake up, you slacker!"

Steve stretched slowly and looked up at the clock. Plopping his head back to the comfort of a pillow, he smiled. "I guess the interview went great."

"No, it was awful. I left there with my head hanging low."

Steve sat back up. "What happened?"

"Well, from the beginning, I could tell there was something wrong. This office didn't look anything like a company that restored historic buildings. If you just walked in off the street, you would have no idea what business they were in. I get into this guy's office ... "

"Summerville ... ?"

Taylor chuckled, "Summerhill. His name was Summerhill. I really scored points when I asked his secretary if I could see Mr. Summerville. Anyway, I get in there and the guy rakes me over the coals. He tells me that Black never intended to tear down the Finck Building. He lectures me on the difficulty of restoring a historic building as if I were some naive college student working on a term paper. Basically, I was handed my pride on a silver platter.

"Anyway, I'm walking out of there and I ask him what other buildings they have restored, and he gives me this vague answer about a handful of properties in Chicago that I probably never heard of. I left there with more questions than answers."

"Did I miss something? You don't seem too disappointed by the events of the morning."

"Because something really amazing happened! I'm walking out of the building, I look up into one of the offices, and who do I run into but a man named Pietr Tzynczynski?"

"Pietr Tzynczynski? Who's that?" asked Steve.

"A name I had never heard of either before Thursday's book signing party. Karl Guenther pulled me aside and told me about the problems he is having with his brother concerning the sale of their ranch. He asked me if I would do a little research into the buyer, who is supposed to be from one of the oldest Polish families in South Texas, descendants of the early settlers in Panna Maria. Well the last thing I need is to take on another research project, but I took the name of the guy who wanted to buy his property anyway. I told him I would look into it and try to smooth things over with his brother ... "

"And this guy's name is Pietr Tzynczynski."

"Exactly. A coincidence?" Taylor asked skeptically. "So I strike up a conversation and tell him that we have a mutual friend, Karl Guenther. And you know what he says? 'Who's Karl Guenther?' I start to wonder if there are two Pietr Tzynczynskis in Texas, and I told him that Karl owned a ranch just north of San Antonio."

"Was it the same Pietr Tzynczynski?"

"Well, that's the weird thing. All of sudden he remembers that he <u>was</u> going to buy a ranch. Don't you think that if you were going to buy someone's ranch that you would remember his name?"

"Yes, you would."

"And the more I talked to him, the more I got the impression that he was trying to remember what the ranch looks like. I asked him a few questions about the place, and he could barely recall what it looks like. In fact, at one point, he started telling me about how he wanted to use the barn to store his classic cars."

Steve quickly chimed in, "That old ranch doesn't have a barn."

"I know," Taylor screamed, barely able to hide his excitement. "Then, it dawned on me. The whole thing started to make sense."

"What? I don't get it."

"Okay. Follow me. We have this company that says it restores historic buildings. But there is only one building we really know that they own. In fact, when it comes to knowing anything about the Brownstone

Company, we come up empty. We've got a business that is privately held, so we know nothing about who owns it or who is on the board of directors. There is no annual report. Then shun any opportunity for publicity. The office is filled with people who look like accountants. Where are the architects, the engineers, the draftsmen?

"And inside the offices is a guy named Pietr Tzynczynski who purchased land recently on the North Side of San Antonio, but he can't even recall what it looks like. He keeps getting it confused with another piece of land. And I ask you my friend, what does all this add up to?"

Steve scratched his head, clearly not following where Taylor was heading. "A poorly run business with a lot of stupid employees?"

"Think again. A company that wants to keep quiet, a company where the employees are buying land, perhaps so much that they can't recall one piece of property from another. What do you think that means?"

Steve shook his head, totally lost, but not without noticing Taylor's excitement.

"Disney, Steve! That company is a front for Disney!"

"Oh my God, Disney! Of course. It makes sense. There has been talk about them buying property around San Antonio for years. It's so perfect. It makes so much sense."

"Exactly! These guys like Pietr Tzynczynski are buying up property under their own names, keeping a low profile. The Brownstone Company is even more secretive, keeping its offices in some nondescript industrial park in Dallas, wanting desperately to keep its name out of the papers."

"How can you be sure, though? I mean, this is so amazing, but it could just be a coincidence."

Taylor's eyes twinkled. "It could very well be a coincidence. That's why I've already devised a plan."

His enthusiasm spread to Steve, who was now fully awake. "Major Taylor! The president of the Travis Club has a plan. Tell me more!" His mocking tone made Taylor laugh.

"While I was in Pietr Tzynczynski's office, this whole Disney thing dawned on me. And I was wondering how I could go about proving this.

"On his desk I saw a sheet of paper with the extensions of everybody who worked in the office. So, I conveniently laid my note pad on top of it when I was talking to him and just picked them both up when I left."

"Major Taylor ... pulling off the heist of the century!"

"As soon as I got out of there, I pulled into a copy shop and called Joe. I told him everything and that I was faxing him a list of names. He, Ted and Ed are going over to the courthouse this morning to see how many pieces of property Mr. Tzynczynski and his cohorts have purchased."

"I can't believe this! Disney coming to San Antonio! But still, a few things don't make sense to me."

Taylor smiled, anticipating the questions. "Such as?"

"Number one, why would the Disney Company be interested in the Finck Cigar Building? And number two, Karl Guenther's ranch is over the aquifer recharge zone. You couldn't develop a humungous place like Disney World there."

"No, you couldn't. But if you look at Disney World in Florida, the actual park is surrounded by acres of natural preserves. That way, the park and the hotels have a natural buffer zone to separate them from the cheap motels, fast food restaurants and strip centers that surround Disneyland in California. The actual park will probably be north of the recharge zone. And as for the Finck Building, they probably picked that up for a song from Black and might use that as a downtown visitor's center, something of that sort."

Steve shook his head in disbelief. "You've really thought this out. This is so amazing. Do you realize how it could change things forever? You know they would be in need of someone like me. I bet I could get a full-time job building floats or working on creating new attractions."

Taylor listened in disbelief as Steve mentioned the possibility of full time employment and realized that it really could change things forever.

* * *

The pair had originally planned to drive home that afternoon but decided that it was not really necessary. After all, neither had a job to get back to. Besides, Steve's brother had invited them out to dinner, and neither felt like turning down a free meal. They had put up with him for four days; one more evening would not matter.

Taylor spent most of the day catching up on his sleep. He tried to call Logan a few times, but she apparently was not back from Houston yet. At about five, Taylor and Steve chose white Salvation Army shirts and ironed them. Steve's brother got home at 5:30 and changed from his tailored suit into a silk shirt with linen slacks and soft leather loafers. A bystander would never guess that the three were going out together. Steve declined a ride in his brother's European sedan because he wanted to stop and have the taco's oil checked before the morning.

Taylor did not relish the ride with Steve's brother because he knew that soon the conversation would turn into an interrogation into Steve's life.

"So, did you get all your work done?" Steve's brother asked, only half interested in an answer.

"Yeah, I worked pretty much nonstop. I really appreciate you letting me crash at your house; It was really a big help."

"No problem. Any friend of Steve's is a friend of mine. He says you had an appointment this morning. Job interview?"

"No, I was ... "—Taylor paused while deciding if he wanted Steve's brother to know the true nature of the appointment—"doing some research on a company that's restoring a historic building in San Antonio."

"Steve says your new book on the Alamo caused quite a stir. It sounds like it's the talk of the town. I've always envied you. I've always wanted to write a book."

When Taylor heard this, he turned his head toward the window and as always, politely replied, "It's not as hard as most people think; you just have to have something to write about. Something you really care about. You have to write what you know."

"I think it's a matter of time. I just don't have the time."

"What did you do last Friday and Saturday night?" Taylor asked.

"I went out to a club."

"Went out to a club. See, you have the time. You just choose to spend it doing something else."

"But, it's a lot easier for you. You don't have a job. I just wish I could spend my whole day at home writing."

"You could if you wanted. Nothing is stopping you from quitting your job and staying home to write, if that's what you really wanted to do."

Steve's brother shook his head, as if to signify that Taylor knew little about the real world. "Like I could just quit my job. I have a mortgage and a car payment that would choke a horse."

"Did someone assign you this car and your house and tell you to pay for them? No. You chose them. It's a lifestyle choice. I chose to live a simpler life, to keep my expenses down so I could spend more time writing. When it comes right down to it, we all have the choice to live whatever kind of life we want."

Steve's brother tightened his grip around the steering wheel. "There used to be a time in this country when a person grew up, accepted some responsibility, and took a job. He felt fortunate to be able to support a family, buy a home, and take a stake in the community. But nowadays it isn't good enough just to have a job. You have to have a 'cool' job."

"A cool job," laughed Taylor. "I prefer to think of it as a job I like. We all have the power to choose our paths in life. If I choose to make my way differently than you, what does it matter? I'm happy with the choices I have made, even if it doesn't bring me great monetary returns. If you hate what you do and don't like the way your life has turned out, only you have the power to change it. And you better make these choices while you still have an opportunity to."

"And Steve, what choices has he made?"

Here was the inevitable question. "What choices has Steve made?"

"Oh, come on. I've been to his place. The guy doesn't even have a TV! He still lives like an impoverished college student. Why does he choose to live like that? Is he sacrificing for some goal? No, not my brother. He is the slacker king. I'm so embarrassed every time I see that giant taco."

"Maybe he likes his lifestyle. Maybe having a TV and a car that doesn't resemble food really means nothing to him. Besides, who is it hurting? It's not like

Steve is on welfare. He pays his own way. He's not always coming to you for money, is he?" Taylor tried to maintain his calm, pausing to sigh. "If anything, it's just the opposite. Your brother is always there when I need a ride to Dallas or something nice to wear to an important meeting."

He relented. "Maybe you're right. After all, it's not like Steve is going down to the Salvation Army and shopping for clothes."

The sedan pulled into the parking lot of the restaurant. Both immediately recognized the giant taco, which seemed so out of place parked next to the expensive sports cars and foreign autos. Taylor noticed Steve's brother wince when he saw it.

Inside, Steve was at the bar talking to a girl in a tight dress. The bar was already filled with young professionals dressed in designer clothes. Steve's brother grabbed a table and the trio sat down. "That girl you were talking to at the bar. I used to date her."

"I know, that's what she said."

His brother's eyes lit up. "Oh really? What did she say?"

"Nothing really. Just that she used to date you." Steve relished the lack of information. Taylor just sat back and watched as the two brothers began their verbal skirmishes. Throughout dinner, his mind drifted back to his troubles in San Antonio. He knew that as soon as he got back, he would have a dozen calls from Father Olivares. Not to mention being followed by Merced, an apartment that had recently been burglarized, no computer, no files and now no job. This trip to Dallas had been an escape for him, a chance to forget his other problems for a few days. But, it was time to get back. He wanted to talk to Father Patrick and see if he had come up with anything more. Plus, there was this Disney business. He could hardly sit still wondering what Joe had discovered.

"Taylor? Taylor ... wake up ... do you want dessert?" Taylor looked at Steve and realized that his mind had been wandering for quite some time. He nodded to the waiter, who promptly left the table.

Steve's brother stood up and announced, "I'm going to go to the bar to say hello to somebody. Why don't you join me?"

"In a second, Taylor and I need to discuss some trip details." The two were left alone. "You can go up to the bar if you want to, but I needed a break from him. Thanks for all your help during dinner. Where was your head?"

Taylor wiped the daze from his eyes, "Was I in another zone or what? I just started thinking about this St. Anthony Retreat mess. As soon as I get back into town, I'll be right back in the middle of it again. Don't forget, if it wasn't for the robbery, we wouldn't have even had to come to Dallas.

"I feel like everybody thinks I own the missing piece to a puzzle and I haven't got a clue what it is that I'm supposed to have. Listen, if you want to go hang out at the bar with your brother, please go ahead. I'll just have some coffee."

Both looked over at the bar, which had become a major center of activity since they had arrived. It was obvious that this was a place to see and be seen. A real poser party, as Joe would have called it.

Steve spotted the girl he had spoken to earlier. She was holding court with a trio of well-dressed young men. Steve's brother was one of them, though the girl was paying little attention to him. "Yes," Steve yawned sarcastically. "I would like nothing more than to hang out with my brother and his disposable friends."

"Disposable friends?"

"Like he cares about these people. All he cares about is letting people know that he used to date that girl in the tight dress. A true friend is one who will chain himself to a toilet with you."

Taylor leaned back in his chair and sipped his coffee. "I wonder if it is too late to get some dessert, a piece of--"

Suddenly his sentence stopped dead as his eyes took over his brain. At the far corner of the restaurant sat Noel Black.

"Steve, don't look right now, but who is that seated at the table in the corner?"

Steve turned around slowly, while Taylor looked away. Quickly turning back he giggled in delight. "Noel Black! It figures he would come to some pretentious Dallasite restaurant like this. We know one thing, he let the valet park his car."

"How do we know that?"

"Major Taylor, you are slipping. Do you think Noel Black would have come in here if he had seen the giant taco in the parking lot? No, he valet parked it." Both were now laughing.

"Look at the people he has at his table. Check out the girl. You know she has to be a heartless gold digger."

Steve turned around to size up the woman that had accompanied Black. Soon, his smile turned sour, his mood turned from ridicule to horror. It was not just any woman with Black.

It was Logan.

"Taylor, maybe we should go hang out at the bar."

Steve's effort to protect him was quickly thwarted. Taylor saw the same thing. His heart began to race. He felt both betrayed and foolish. How could he let this happen to himself? He sat frozen in his chair.

Finally, Taylor could take no more. "Let's get out of here." In his haste to exit, he ran into a dessert cart, knocking portions of cheesecake and sherbet about. The entire restaurant went silent and all eyes were focused on him. He looked up straight into Logan's eyes for a split second.

Time stood still. They both knew the same thing at the same instant. He had been betrayed, and her game was over.

Taylor ran from the restaurant with raspberry cheesecake topping stuck to his shirt. The eyes of the restaurant shifted to Steve. "Excuse us, my friend is deathly allergic to cheesecake."

Outside, he saw Taylor kicking a plaster tomato off the taco car. Steve rushed to save him from destroying the creation. Steve grabbed him and buried his head into his shoulder. "Let's go home, Major."

Steve opened the car door and Taylor sunk inside. Defeated, betrayed, angry and hurt, he realized that he had just made his first disposable friend.

Chapter 19

The clock had barely struck 4:00 a.m. when the taco car pulled into city limits. A delivery truck for the Alamo Ice Company honked to salute the vehicle as it entered San Antonio, waking Steve, who had slept most of the way.

Taylor had accepted a rare second chance to drive the taco, knowing that he would not be able to sleep. When they arrived at the Floraman house, he offered Steve the use of the couch, realizing that his traveling partner was not fully awake. Before going to the bedroom, he checked his phone messages. There were five frantic messages from Father Olivares and one from a local bookstore asking him to set up a book signing.

As soon as Taylor got into his own bed and his head hit the pillow, his eyes slammed shut. Mr. Tibbs curled up near his feet and purred contentedly. But, for Taylor, sleep was anything but content. All he could see in his dreams was that stare. The locking gaze that he shared with Logan, lasting only a second but speaking volumes.

His tossing and turning was interrupted at 10:00 a.m., when Eric Bob threw a pillow at him. "Are you going to sleep your life away?"

Rubbing the sleep from his eyes, Taylor sat up and squinted toward his friend. "What are you doing here?"

"You asked me to feed Mr. Tibbs. Besides, I should be asking you what you're doing home. I was a bit surprised to see the taco car outside this morning."

Taylor sighed and lay back down. "There wasn't much reason for us to stay any longer."

"Steve told me. Talk about a bad week. You lost your job, your home was broken into, and your computer and your files were stolen. Not to mention that your truck will probably never run again and the Catholic diocese thinks you're a modern-day Judas and has someone following you. On top of all that, you find out that your new girlfriend is just pretending to like you but in reality she is quite friendly with Noel Black."

Taylor buried his head in his pillow. "Are you done cheering me up?"

"Not yet; I have a couple of bits of news that should make you feel better. First of all, Joe asked me to bring you over to his office. He says that he has some news for you."

"What! News from Joe?" Taylor leapt from the bed, grabbed a pair of shorts, and threw them on. He raced toward the closet and pulled a clean t-shirt from the top shelf. "This is great! Did he say anything else?"

"No, he just said to get you and bring you back to his office. What is all this about?"

"Big news, Eric Bob! Wake Steve up and tell him that we need to go."

"He's already gone. He went home to clean up, and he said he would meet us there. Is somebody going to tell me what's going on?"

Taylor sucked on the end on an empty toothpaste tube, trying to deliver the last bit onto his teeth. "We need to get out of here." Giving up on the toothpaste, he slid his wet toothbrush across a bar of soap and lathered up his teeth. Grimacing, he spat out suds, rinsed his mouth, and splashed warm water onto his face. "Can you give me a ride to Joe's office?"

"Yeah, I guess so, since that is one of the reasons I came over here. Maybe you can fill me in on what the big deal is."

Taylor yanked a pair of sneakers onto his feet, bypassing socks. "I'll tell you in the car." Halfway out the front door he looked back at Eric Bob. "You just going to sit there? Let's go!"

* * *

As they raced to Joe's office, Taylor relived the tale of visiting the Brownstone headquarters, running into Pietr Tzynczynski, and coming up with the Disney connection.

"What does this have to do with Joe?"

"I faxed back a copy of a list of employees of the Brownstone Company. He, Ted, and Ed are checking the county courthouses to see how many pieces of property the so-called Brownstone employees have been purchasing. It looks like he has some news."

The two arrived at Joe's office slightly after Steve did. The offices looked more like a house than a place of business. At one time the street had been home to stately residences of the city's German elite. But eventually the neighborhood fell into disrepair, and the homes were torn down or made into offices. Joe's old building was the most recently renovated on the street.

When Taylor walked in, he could tell that his encounter with Logan was the topic of conversation. Joe, Ted, Ed, and a new law clerk were huddled around Steve, who was telling everybody how he had announced to the entire restaurant that his friend was allergic to cheesecake. As soon as Taylor walked in, the concerned eyes turned to him as if he were in an aquarium.

"Please don't stop on my account! I want the world to know how I was made a fool of."

Joe strode over and pulled him into the conference room. "Don't let this get to you," he said quietly. "Be flattered that Black would consider you such a threat that he would send a beautiful woman to betray you. Kind of sounds like a James Bond thing, doesn't it?"

"Great, I was made a fool of by Pussy Galore. That makes me feel a whole lot better."

"See, I knew that I could help." Joe put his arm around him and led him upstairs to his office. "Enough of this, anyway. We have much more to worry about this morning ... Mr. Disney!"

Taylor's mood immediately improved. "Did you find something? Was I right?"

"The great Major Taylor. You were both right and wrong at the same time. You had the right address, but you were knocking at the wrong door."

The whole group followed Joe upstairs and into his office. The room, the largest in the old home, had a balcony and a sitting room that he used as a private conference area. Before closing the door, Joe asked his clerk to go downstairs and keep an eye on the place.

"Yesterday, Ted, Ed and I went to the county archives," Joe began. "Your buddy Mr. Meachum is getting sick of seeing us."

"We divided the list by three, each taking seven names. We started searching for every title that has been transferred to one of these names. The results are shocking." Joe wheeled out a bulletin board and turned it toward his audience. "We highlighted in green the pieces of property that were purchased by people on my list. The number in the center corresponds with a name on the list. Ted's list is highlighted in blue, Ed's in yellow."

As the county map came in view of the club members, their mouths dropped. The northern portion of the map looked like a checkerboard done in highlighted colors.

"Unbelievable!" gasped Steve. "Looks like they already own a third of the north part of the county!"

"And this is just what we've found so far," reminded Joe. "We've only searched back a year. There is no telling how long this has been going on."

"I'm surprised that no one has caught on," Eric Bob said. "That much property being sold, you think somebody would have noticed."

"Remember that each of these colors represents the efforts of seven different people," Ed said.

"Yeah, and that's the edge of the hill country. It's pretty isolated out there," Ted added. "Our Uncle Karl knows his immediate neighbors and that's about it."

Taylor remained silent while the others closely observed the map and made their comments. "It seems like these different parcels are pretty spread out. It doesn't look like a Disney project, does it, Joe?"

"I was thinking the exact same thing. Last night I was putting this map together, and it occurred to me that this land is a lot more spread out. I also noticed that it appears to be in clusters." He walked up to the easel and motioned to an area near the top. "Look here, it seems that a lot of this property is centered around this little lake. Then over here is a bunch of property near the highway. Then, a third cluster of land is near the old gravel pits. Not one large Disney World-type development, but three very separate groups of property.

"So I started looking into the titles and I noticed that they were all financed through a company called Western Financial."

"Western Financial?" Eric Bob asked.

"Yes, and for some reason that name struck a chord with me. Then, I remembered, aren't they the holding company that purchased Alamo National Bank last year? Anyway, I did a little checking this morning, and guess who is on the board of Western Financial?"

"Let me guess," chimed in Steve, who knew everybody had the same thought. "Noel Black."

"Exactly. And Edward Summerhill of the Brownstone Company," Joe added. Silence fell upon the room as everyone contemplated the consequences.

"Western Financial ... " Ted muttered. "I didn't know that was the company that bought the Alamo National Bank. Isn't that where Logan worked?" Everybody stared at him and then at Taylor, who buried his head into his hands.

Eric Bob sat down and cleared his disc jockey's voice. "You want more bad news? Remember how the owners of WOAI just purchased three new radio stations across Texas? Guess who financed that loan? Western Financial."

"The bank puts a little pressure on the station, and the next thing you know, Taylor is gone." Silence filled the room. It felt like the whole club had just gotten blindsided. Everybody stared at Taylor, looking for leadership.

Finally the young scribe got up and looked out the window. "Guys, this is a nightmare."

Steve turned away and began restudying the map. "I don't get it, I just don't get it. I've been out to Karl's ranch a million times. Why would anyone want to buy all that property? The potential for development is limited with it sitting over the aquifer recharge zone."

"At the present time it is." Joe corrected. "Don't you see? He is buying all this property on speculation while the prices are low. He's hoping that someday he'll be able to develop the land and make a killing."

"And he wants to make sure that we don't get in the way. That's why he's trying to silence us by getting Taylor fired. And he sent Logan here to spy on us. The potential for profits is huge"

Taylor remained at the window, staring outside. "There is more to this than meets the eye. There is a missing piece to the puzzle, and it all has to do with the St. Anthony retreat."

"I don't know," Joe said. "The retreat is on the other side of the county. How can all this be tied together?"

"I don't know either, but both Father Olivares and Noel Black believe I have the missing piece to this puzzle, or at least have access to it. And they both are very scared that with this missing piece, I could ruin them. One of them broke into my house and stole everything I had written. And Noel Black is so scared that he sends Logan here to spy on us, and he leaves me without a job. Too many coincidences. The answer exists somewhere at that retreat. But what is it?"

Suddenly Eric Bob leapt on his chair. "I know somebody who can help us! Who designed the St. Anthony Retreat?"

The club was in little mood to amuse him. Finally Steve spoke, "Randall Hugley."

"And who is the foremost expert on the life of Randall Hugley?" Seeing that he was losing the crowd, he answered his own question. "Our own Taylor Nichols, who wrote a very splendid book on the life of one Randall Hugley. But, great Major Taylor, I reread your effort last night and your book had one glaring error!"

Taylor turned from the window, in no mood for fun and games. "And what would that be?"

"You wrote that Randall Hugley was dead, but you're wrong!"

"What?"

"Randall Hugley is alive. Alive and living in California."

Chapter 20

"Impossible," Taylor said, shaking his head.

"Impossible, no. Incredible, yes." Eric Bob perched on the arm of a large leather chair, clearly relishing his command of the room.

"What are you talking about?" asked Taylor, filled with new intrigue.

"Saturday, after you got the axe and left the station, I got stuck running the board for the world's most boring two hours of radio, known as the WOAI *Radio Kitchen*. I'm there, screening the calls. Most of them are complaint calls wondering what happened to Taylor's show. After about an hour of this, I get a call from Stewart."

"Who's Stewart?" asked Joe, who had pulled up a chair and was listening intently.

"Stewart is this guy who called my show every week," Taylor said slowly. "He's been living here forever and always gives me these great leads. He's the one that tipped me off to the bogus Davy Crockett tomb."

"Only, Stewart's call was different. He wasn't complaining about the show being canceled; he was calling to ask a question. He didn't realize that you weren't even on the air."

"Maybe he's just senile. You said he was an old guy," offered Steve.

"No, this guy's not senile; he's too sharp," answered Eric Bob. "When I told him the show had been canceled, all I heard was silence, then he hung up. I got a little worried, so I checked the caller ID."

"What's caller ID?" said a surprised Taylor.

"It's not something that we're supposed to tell the talk show hosts about. They installed the system about a week ago, one of those new phone company options. It displays the phone number of every caller. Someday it will be available in homes, but right now it's only accessible to a few select businesses. If a talk show host gets a threatening call, we are supposed to check the caller ID and find a number, then notify police."

"I get it. That keeps us hosts in the dark about threatening calls."

"Exactly, so as not to worry you. See, management was looking out for you before they canned you." The comment brought laughter at Taylor's expense.

"Anyway," Eric Bob continued, "the number on caller ID had a Los Angeles area code."

"Los Angeles?" asked Joe. "Sounds like a mistake."

"That's what I thought, but I decided to call the number anyway."

"And Randall Hugley answered," offered Joe, who thought he was one step ahead.

"No, it was a nursing home. Some type of retirement center. Something like that. I asked if there was a person named Stewart there, and the nurse said they had no one by that name."

"Was it Hugley who was really making all those calls?" Joe interrupted again.

"Yes, but I didn't find out until last night."

"Incredible," said Joe, speaking as if he were before a jury. "But, how did you figure out that it was Hugley who was really making those calls to you?"

"Good question, counsel," mocked Eric Bob, amused by Joe's courtroom demeanor. "I was wondering all weekend about this Stewart guy. Why would some guy from a California nursing home be calling a radio show in San Antonio? Then I thought back to some of the 'helpful leads' Stewart had given Taylor over the years. Such as the last one, when he told you that the Alamo Tomb might be a fraud. I wondered how he knew so much about that.

"So, I followed a hunch. I got out a copy of your new book and looked at a list of every name that was present the day they uncovered those remains. All prominent San Antonians. All passed away. But there was one name that troubled me, Randall Hugley.

"I remember when you wrote his biography. You had trouble finding out anything about the final part of his life, including when and where he died. I was there when you asked Mrs. Floraman if she knew what happened to him, and she said that she had heard he died years ago. I remember how you just left it vague, since you were never really able to confirm it.

"It was just a hunch, so last night I called the nursing home back and asked if I could speak to Randall Hugley."

"Did you?" questioned Joe.

"He was already asleep. But he was there. He is alive."

"Remind me not to have you write my biography," Steve joked to Taylor.

Noticing that Taylor had remained quiet throughout the story, Eric Bob opened his wallet and handed him a piece of paper. "I thought about calling back this morning, but I figured you should be the one to talk to him."

"What is he going to tell him? 'Hi, my name is Taylor Nichols; I wrote a book about your life but thought you were dead?'" Steve cut himself off, realizing his jokes were not appreciated.

"I was right out of college when I wrote that book. Maybe I wasn't as thorough as I should have been. Regardless, I have been given a very special gift, a chance to talk with someone I admire and wrote about, someone I thought was dead and someone who can help me solve the enigma that my life has become and answer some questions about the St. Anthony Retreat. Joe, may I use your phone?"

"Go right ahead."

Taylor's hand trembled as he dialed. He sat down and waited for the ring. It was busy.

* * *

After spending the afternoon at the county courthouse searching for further Brownstone acquisitions, Taylor decided to stop by St. Agnes to visit Father Patrick. A few minutes early, he hung out across the street in a pharmacy waiting for 5:30 confession to begin. He wanted to go early and check out those candlesticks made from old Alamo rifles, but he hated to burst into the sanctuary unannounced. Sipping lemonade and picking at a piece of pecan pie, Taylor waited until 5:45 before paying his tab, then cautiously crossed the street and entered the church. He had already become much less cavalier about his own safety, considering that his house had been broken into, this Merced character had been following him and he had learned that Logan had been really spying on him. He decided to adopt a few new precautions when it came to visiting St. Agnes. The last thing he wanted was to cause trouble between the diocese and this small neighborhood parish.

He slipped into an open confessional and the priest opened the screen. "Bless me, father, it has been about a week since I've talked to you. I hoped you enjoyed the book."

"Taylor! So nice of you to visit. I heard from the Guenthers that you had a break-in."

"Father, that's just a small part of an unbelievable week. And, somehow, everything seems to tie in to the retreat."

"I'm listening."

"Last Thursday I got back to my apartment and the place had been trashed. They stole all my files, my Hugley drawings, my computer...everything."

"Whom do you suspect?"

"At first I thought it was Merced and Father Olivares. But it could have just as easily been Black. One thing is for sure, they were looking for those drawings and they didn't find them. They took everything, including some rewrites I had for an updated version of an old book. I had to go to Dallas to recover my files and to rewrite the updates."

"I trust you kept your Sunday obligation while in Dallas?"

Taylor recognized the priest's sarcasm and let it pass. He proceeded to fill in the rest of the blanks, including his trip to the Brownstone offices, his incorrect Disney assumption, the Noel Black connection, and of course, his episode with Logan. He finally topped off his tale with Eric Bob's discovery that Randall Hugley was alive.

The father listened in the darkness of the confessional, taking all this in. The story seemed almost too incredible to be true. "How can you be so sure that this land on the North Side is somehow connected to the retreat?" he finally asked.

Taylor knew it must sound strange. But, he just had a gut feeling that all this was intertwined. And even if it wasn't, it did not really matter. That Black was secretly buying land in the recharge area and desperately looking for plans to the retreat were both facts that concerned him. Explaining all this to the priest, though, made him feel like a mobile home owner who had seen a UFO.

"What's your next step?" Father Patrick asked.

"First of all, I'm going to try to contact Hugley," Taylor said. "If anybody can fill me in on why this retreat is so damn important, it's the guy who built it. After that, I'm just playing it by ear."

"Be careful, my son. Word has gotten around the diocese that Father Olivares is desperate. The bishop is extremely upset about the sale of the retreat. The Father must make amends."

"What I don't understand is why it matters to them to have the plans to the retreat. What difference does that make? But now, I have an edge. I know the one person with the answer."

"Randall Hugley is obviously your ace in the hole. I suggest you call him as soon as possible. He's rather old."

"I'll call as soon as I get home," Taylor replied, wondering how the priest knew that Hugley was 'rather old.'

* * *

Taylor began striding up the back stairs to his apartment, but stopped halfway up. Mr. Tibbs was already waiting at the window in anticipation when Taylor turned, jaunted back down, and knocked on Mrs. Floraman's door. She smiled instantly upon seeing him.

"I figured you had come back from Dallas. I saw that giant taco pull up this morning, but you were gone before I got a chance to come up and see you."

"I had some business to attend to. A lot is happening."

"I'll say! Every time I turn on the TV there is another story about Davy Crockett's tomb. You're not in trouble with the church, are you?"

"Not really."

"I hope not. You've had two visits from some priest from the bishop's office since you were gone. Whatever it was sounded urgent."

"Was it a Father Olivares?"

"That's him. He's got those cold steely eyes. Remind me never to go to confession when he is in the booth. He looks like he'd give you a thousand Hail Marys for saying 'shit.'"

Taylor, taken aback by her candor, suppressed a chuckle. He took her hand and led the woman into her living room. The smell of witch hazel and lace filled the air. "Mrs. Floraman, I have some news. It's rather shocking, but I thought you may want to know."

"Taylor, you're in trouble, aren't you?"

"No, it's not that kind of news. It's good news. Please ... sit down." Taylor pulled up an old wooden stool next to the leather chair that she had sunk into. "I know how fond you were of Randall Hugley. And I know how heartbroken you were to have lost touch with him.

"Mrs. Floraman, he's alive and living in California. He never passed away."

The old woman slumped into her chair. Her eyes sunk and she gasped, "What?"

Taylor proceeded to recount to her how Eric Bob had discovered that the architect and former tenant was still living and residing in a nursing home in Los Angeles. "We tried to contact him this morning, but we could never make a connection. I'm going to go upstairs now and try to get through. Why don't you come with me and--"

"NO!" she interrupted. "Leave him alone. Don't bother the man." Taylor was struck by the strong reaction. She rose from her chair and grabbed his shoulders. "Promise me, Taylor, promise me that you won't try to contact him." He mumbled something about the St. Anthony Retreat, but his words fell unheard. "Why can't you leave things alone? Why must you always be snooping into the past? Some things were meant to be forgotten."

The young man sat, dumbfounded. "I thought you would be pleased to know--"

"Pleased? Promise me that you won't contact him. Please don't bring shame into my life." Tears began to drop onto her cheeks. Taylor tried to calm her, but he avoided making any promises. He knew deep down that he could not pass up a chance to talk to the legendary architect. Her pleas became more desperate. "Don't do this to me. Just let me be." She turned, ran to her bedroom and slammed the door. . "Don't bring shame into my life!"

He stood outside her bedroom and pleaded with her to open the door. The only answer was sobbing. Deciding that further efforts were futile, he walked to the back door and exited, making sure that her gray cat did not go outside.

Taylor looked at the clock, suddenly realizing how late it was in the afternoon. He took the number out of his pocket and dialed. Mentally, he subtracted two hours, figuring that this would be a good time to call Los Angeles, as if one time would be better than another for a man in his 80s.

After four rings, a harried voice answered. "Hello, St. Peter's Retirement Center."

"Yes, I was hoping to speak with a Mr. Randall Hugley."

The attendant on the other end paused. "I'm sorry, but Mr. Hugley suffered a stroke this morning. He was taken earlier today--"

"Taken?" Taylor's demeanor quickly changed from excited to desperate. "What do you mean, taken?"

The nurse spoke in a detached tone, "This morning he was taken to Sacred Hearts Hospital."

"What kind of condition is he in? How serious was the stroke? Was this his first stroke?" Taylor reeled off the questions.

The nurse tried to maintain her cool, but was clearly losing patience with the call. "Sir, I am just an employee here at the nursing home. Mr. Hugley left this morning and is now under the care of the doctors at Sacred Hearts Hospital. I suggest that you call there and inquire as to his condition. I have very little information here."

Taylor forced himself to calm down, realizing that the nurse was not the reason for his frustration. "You're right. I'm sorry, it was just a bit of a shock to call and find out that he had suffered a stroke." He asked for the hospital's number and hung up.

Quickly, he dialed Sacred Hearts, deciding to use a different tack. "Hello, I'm calling from San Antonio, Texas, to find out the condition of a relative of mine, Randall Hugley. He was admitted this morning with a stroke."

"One moment, please." He was put on hold. Minutes passed and his mind drifted to Mrs. Floraman. Should he tell her about the stroke or should he just leave her alone? Her reaction had left him confused, and he decided to just drop it. It would only make it worse. "Hello, sir? I'm going to transfer you to Intensive Care." The phone clicked over and was quickly answered.

"Intensive Care, were you the one inquiring about Mr. Hugley?"

"Yes."

"His condition has been downgraded to serious. He is still not out of the woods. Hopefully, he'll be able to be moved from ICU by early next week."

"Early next week?"

"The stroke was rather serious, plus we are talking about a man in his 80s. He may never fully recover."

"I guess talking to him on the phone is out of the question. I'm calling from San Antonio."

"There is no way he can talk on the phone in his condition. But immediate family members are allowed short supervised visitations from 11:00 a.m. to noon daily. I'm sorry, how did you say you were related to Mr. Hugley?"

"I'm his nephew," Taylor bluffed. "We were very close."

"The only thing that I can tell you is that if you are in the Los Angeles area, you can come by during visitations. Like I said, he is in his 80s and he may never fully recover."

Taylor thanked her and put down the receiver. He was too late. If he were closer, he could stop by and visit, but jumping on a plane at the last minute and flying to Los Angeles was out of his price range. He could wait a week and see if Hugley was transferred out of intensive care, but Taylor knew that he really did not have a week to spare. Besides, what could he do? Drive to California with Steve in a giant taco? The idea of being some type of freakish Joad family neither appealed to him nor seemed too practical.

He could ask one of the other Travis Club members for the money, but he knew none of them would have enough. If only there was a way ...

Something in the corner of the room caught his eye: a white shirt that Steve had taken off and thrown there that morning before catching a few Zs on the couch.

"The white shirt!" he said to Mr. Tibbs, who had fallen asleep on the garment. The cat jumped up, startled at his tone, and scrambled toward the kitchen. Taylor raced after him and brought him back to Steve's crumpled shirt. "Not that one, the one with the giant hole." The cat lay back down on his domain and watched as Taylor started to tear through a hamper of dirty clothes. He was on a mission to find that torn shirt. "Did I give it back to Steve?" he wondered.

That was his biggest fear now. If he had returned it, there was a chance that his buddy had already dropped it off at the Salvation Army to be cleaned and pressed. He dialed Steve's number.

"Hello?"

"Hey, this is Taylor. Did I give you back that white shirt that I used for my book signing party?"

"The one with the hole? Let me check." Taylor crossed his fingers and tried to ignore thoughts of he and Steve picking through piles of white shirts at Salvation Army headquarters, looking for the Holy Grail; *the* holey shirt. "Found it." Steve answered. "I must have taken it home by mistake this morning. It's not like I wanted it back."

"Look in the pocket! What's in the pocket?"

"Cool your jets." Steve put the phone down and looked into the pocket. "There's nothing but a credit card receipt." Suddenly, Steve laughed. "What are you going to do with this?"

"Just give me the number and the expiration date."

* * *

Twenty minutes later, Taylor had told Steve the story of his conversation with Mrs. Floraman and

Randall Hugley's stroke. After they hung up, Taylor paged through the phone book and dialed again.

"Hello, Republic Airlines."

"Yes, I would like to book a seat on the first flight to Los Angeles," he began.

"How would you like to pay for this, sir?"

"I'll put it on my credit card."

"I'll need your number, the expiration date, and the name as it appears on the card."

Taylor cleared his throat. "The name is Noel Black."

Chapter 21

Taylor leaned back in the chair and closed his eyes. A flight attendant approached him and asked if he wanted anything to drink. She hung around for a few minutes, inquiring about the purpose of his trip. Taylor sensed that she was flirting, but he was too inept with women to even know where to begin. Joe always said jokingly that he was "not very handy with the ladies."

He had arrived in San Antonio less than a day ago and was already off again. Even though the purpose of his trip could prove to be extremely illuminating, he was a bit disappointed to be leaving again. His newest book on the Alamo was causing quite a stir, and he had to turn down many requests for interviews. He consoled himself with the theory that by being so seemingly elusive, he might create even more interest in the book.

Taylor had used that theory on Kirk, who blew a fuse when he found out that Taylor was going to L.A. and did not know how long he would be there. Taylor had bought two sets of tickets to Los Angeles using Noel Black's credit card. One left that evening and returned the next night. The other left San Antonio two days later and returned in a week. The purpose of all the tickets was really quite simple. He did not know how long he would have to stay on the West Coast. If Randall Hugley was in good enough shape to talk to him tomorrow, then he would return tomorrow night. If Hugley was unable to communicate with him right away, Taylor could stay up to a week. He hoped this would not be the case, because he had not really thought about how he would pay for a place to stay.

The second ticket from San Antonio to L.A. was just a ploy so as not to create suspicion with the airline. He felt bad enough buying two tickets, but at least they were both coach. He had thought about flying first class but decided not to go overboard.

He did splurge and have the tickets couriered to a fictitious address for an additional twenty dollars. This allowed him to bypass going to the ticket counter at the airport and having them ask for the actual credit card, which of course he did not have. He asked that the tickets be sent to his San Antonio office in the very prestigious Tower Life Building. Because it was after five, the package could be left with the night watchman, who would hold it for him. The airline might have been surprised to learn that its customer would arrive at the airport in a giant taco.

The hum of the jet's engines relaxed him as his eyes grew heavy. Twenty-four hours ago he had been in Dallas. Since then, he had made three important discoveries. The first, he was flying to Los Angeles to learn more about Randall Hugley. Second, Joe and the Guenther brothers discovered that the shadow Brownstone Company was much more extensive than they had first imagined. The further back they checked, the more they revealed. The Brownstone's acquisitions were larger than they had originally thought.

The third discovery was the disappointing news about Logan. After he had made his plane reservations and called Joe to fill him in, he received a call from her. When he heard her voice, he hung up. He did not want an explanation. It was too obvious. He didn't care to hear any more lies. He decided it would be best if he just swore off women for a while.

Too wired to sleep, he pulled out a copy of the local newspaper. After dissecting the sports section, he combed through the local pages. A story about a teacher at a Catholic school on the border caught his eye. Apparently, a church investigator had determined that the teacher had molested a child. According to the story, church spokesman Father Olivares believed that the church dealt with the problem in a timely manner.

Taylor read the story twice before falling asleep.

* * *

"Sir, we've landed." The flight attendant who had welcomed Taylor earlier reached over and gently nudged him. He awoke to find that the plane had landed and he was one of the last people on board.

He looked out the window and could see that it was morning. He figured that he had been sleeping for some time by the taste in his mouth. The young lady smiled at him. "Perhaps you would like to freshen up a bit before you leave?"

Taylor went into the compact bathroom and splashed some water on his face. He put a little soap on his finger and attempted to brush his teeth. He had left in such a hurry the night before that he had neglected to pack anything, including a toothbrush. The taste of airline soap lasted only seconds before he spit it out. It was more than he could stand. He vainly attempted to comb his hair but it seemed useless. He emerged to find the attendant stowing blankets in the overhead compartment. "Pardon me, ma'am?" he said meekly.

"Kim," she answered. "You can call me Kim."

"All right, Kim. I need to get to Sacred Hearts Hospital. It's near downtown Los Angeles. What would be the best way of getting there?"

"You could take a cab; that would run about 50 dollars." She saw him grimace and realized that that was a bit too expensive. "You could take a shuttle for about 25 dollars."

"I was kind of hoping to take a city bus."

"Have you ever been to Los Angeles before? Nobody takes the city bus. I wouldn't even begin to know how to tell you to get there. Besides, you don't want to take your luggage on a bus. It would get stolen."

"Well, I don't have any luggage."

Her smile disappeared. The whole night she thought she might be flirting with someone special. Now he just seemed more like an airline stowaway. "May I ask why you are in L.A.?"

Taylor wondered how much he should tell her and how much she really cared to hear. "Someone very important in my life had a stroke yesterday, and I've traveled all night to see him. I jumped on the plane with very little money and no luggage, and I'm just trying to get to Sacred Hearts Hospital as cheaply as possible."

The smile returned to her face. "Listen, I shouldn't be doing this, but I could give you a ride to the hospital."

"Are you sure it's not out of your way?" Taylor said, careful not to object too much.

"We'll make a deal. I'll take you to the hospital, and the next time I'm in San Antonio you can take me out to dinner on the River Walk. I've always loved that city."

"It's a deal," he replied, handing her a card with his phone number. "I know that city better than anybody."

"Taylor Nichols," she read from her card. "That sounds like the name of the guy who wrote my boring college textbook."

* * *

Sacred Hearts Hospital was a confusing maze of clinics, laboratories, wings, halls, and rooms. A nurse told Taylor to follow the yellow line to the west wing and then the blue line to intensive care. Taylor figured he might have better luck if he just went to the outside of the building, walked through the emergency door, and found the ICU that way.

A half hour and three orderlies later he finally located the unit. He checked the clock and saw that it was only 9:15 a.m., still an hour and forty-five minutes before visiting hours. He decided it would not do any harm to inquire on Hugley's condition and maybe, if he was lucky, be able to visit early.

"Excuse me," he said to the nurse in charge. "I just flew in from San Antonio and was wondering if you could tell me the condition of Randall Hugley?"

The nurse barely glanced up from her paperwork and asked who he was inquiring about. "Randall Hugley. I was told he was in intensive care last night and that he would most likely be still here this morning. I just flew in this morning from ... "

The nurse closed her clipboard hurriedly and excused herself. "Let me get the doctor, one moment please."

Taylor turned his head away from the nurses' stand and looked through a glass window at a patient hooked up to a variety of life support systems. He wondered what devices Randall Hugley would be attached to. He began to think that his stay in Los Angeles might be longer than anticipated.

"Hello, I'm Dr. Bloomquist," came a booming, reassuring voice behind him. "I was told that you were here to inquire about Mr. Hugley."

"Yes, I flew in from San Antonio this morning to visit."

The doctor asked him to sit down. "I'm sorry, but Mr. Hugley passed away during the night. We did everything we could. I'm sorry that no one contacted you. Perhaps you were in transit."

Taylor slumped down in the cheap vinyl lounger. "He's gone?"

"Again, let me express my regrets. I'm sorry no one from the family contacted you." The doctor sat down beside him and put an arm on his shoulder. Taylor fought to hold back his tears. "Mr. Hugley just wasn't strong enough to recover from a stroke of that magnitude. He died peacefully."

The tears began to fall down the young writer's cheeks. He continued the losing battle to hold his emotions in check.

The doctor reached into his pocket and handed Taylor a tissue. "Perhaps you would like to visit our chapel."

"I barely found this place, I doubt I could find your chapel," Taylor joked in a vain attempt to cover his pain. "If I could have some time alone to collect myself." The doctor complied with his wishes and left him to himself. Taylor went around the corner, found a couch behind a soda machine and let the tears run freely. He did not even know why he was crying. Was it because of the passing of a man whom he admired but had never met? Perhaps, but he had only learned that the architect was alive the day before. Maybe it had more to do with the pain and frustration of the last week and a half. He had come so close to finding some answers, but it had all slipped through his hands. He hoped that his tears were not for selfish reasons, but he was so confused he could not really tell. He sat there alone and lost track of the time.

"Pardon me," interrupted a stranger, "but Doctor Bloomquist told me that you were here to see my father-in-law?"

Taylor looked up and wiped away his tears. 'Did he say father-in-law?' he asked himself. Did Randall Hugley have a daughter? Some biographer, he thought. "Is your father-in-law Randall Hugley?"

"Yes," answered the man who appeared to be in his mid-fifties. "I'm David Whitehall. I don't believe we have ever met." His demeanor was quite pleasant considering that some stranger was in a hospital to see his deceased father-in-law.

"I'm Taylor Nichols, I'm from San Antonio. I wrote a ... "

"A biography on Randall," Whitehall interrupted. "It is a pleasure to meet you."

"You know of me?" The writer asked, both surprised and flattered.

"Well, not really," The gray haired man said sheepishly, trying not to burst the young writer's bubble. "But my father-in-law was apparently a big fan of yours. He read all your books.

"As for myself and my wife, I must confess that we had never heard of you until this morning."

"Until this morning?"

"Yes. As you know, Randall passed away last night. His stroke was quite severe. According to his wishes, we read the will as soon as possible. His estate was not that substantial. Curiously, at the end of the reading, the lawyer produced a package that was to be delivered to you immediately after his death with explicit instructions that only you were to review the materials enclosed.

"Neither my wife nor myself had any idea who you were. We were quite shocked when the lawyer produced a copy of your biography. It was like another life of my father-in-law's was revealed to us. We had no idea of the work he had accomplished in San Antonio."

"You mean you had no idea that he had designed the River Walk or some of the city's more important buildings?"

"The Randall Hugley I knew and the one you wrote about were two different men. I knew a devoted father whose daughter came first and his work second. The

Randall Hugley I knew worked mainly designing private homes. We never knew the scale of his work until today when we were going over your book."

"This is unbelievable. It was not until last night that I even realized that he was still alive. As you may have noticed from the biography, I thought he had died years ago."

"Randall obviously knew of your book and did nothing to correct the assumption that he died. For some reason he wanted his San Antonio life and his one in California kept apart. It was his life, and we respect his wishes.

"Regardless, there is a package for you at my lawyer's office. Would you like to have it now or would you rather have it delivered to you in San Antonio as originally planned?"

"I came all this way for some answers. I'll take whatever I can get."

"Answers?" asked the son-in-law. "Answers to what?"

* * *

As the pair exited the hospital and drove through
the maze of L.A. streets to a tall, steely office building
in the center of downtown, Taylor filled in the details of
his own life and how it had dovetailed with Randall
Hugley's. He explained how he lived in Hugley's old
upstairs apartment, had found his drawings, and had
written his biography. He relayed the tale of the St.
Anthony Retreat, the Noel Black land grab, the interest
of the Catholic diocese in the drawings, and the strange
turn of events that led him to the Los Angeles hospital.
David Whitehall listened and drove, thinking to himself
how amazing it was that the early life of his father-in-
law still touched people almost half a century later.

The pair pulled into a parking garage and took an
elevator to the 11th floor. They exited into the lobby of
a well-furnished firm. Taylor thought to himself how
different this was from the refurbished house that
served as Joe's office.

David gave the lawyer's name to the young lady at the reception desk, and the two were promptly led back to an office to greet an attorney in a tailored suit.

"Mr. Whitehall, welcome. I didn't expect to see you again today."

"I didn't expect to return so soon. I went back to the hospital to collect Randall's effects and I ran into this gentleman. Meet Taylor Nichols."

The lawyer's mouth dropped as he stared at the young man standing in front of him. Earlier today, he had wondered who this writer was and how difficult it would be to find him. And now, Taylor Nichols was before him. All he could say was, "I have a package for you."

Taylor walked up and shook the hand of the lawyer, who was struggling to compose himself. "That's what I came for."

"Of course you did." The attorney buzzed his secretary and asked her to bring in the package for Taylor Nichols. He then pointed to a seat and asked the two guests to sit down. "I'm going to need to see a couple of pieces of I.D. I'm sorry, but it is just standard procedure. Anybody can just walk off the street and say that they are you."

"Yeah, but until today, who would want to?" joked Taylor. He reached into his pocket and pulled out his wallet. Having only a driver's license and no credit cards, he searched for a second form of identification. After a few moments he took a card out. It was the first time he had ever used his library card for identification.

Chapter 22

The doors of the huge conference room shut behind Taylor, left alone with his package. He appreciated the lawyer's offer to view the materials in private, but he knew that David Whitehall was waiting for him and he could not take too much time. He thought maybe it would be better to wait and open this in San Antonio in front of the other members of the Travis Club, but his curiosity was too intense.

The package had obviously been rewrapped for delivery. Using a pocket knife that the lawyer had supplied, he sloppily stripped off the tape and opened it in haste. Atop a heap of Styrofoam filler lay a legal size envelope. On the outside were the typed words, "To Taylor Nichols; from Randall Hugley." This time, Taylor took care in unsealing the envelope and extracting the letter. He sat in one of the conference room chairs and unfolded the paper. His hands trembled as he read.

Dear Taylor,

By now my lawyers have contacted and informed you that for the past many years I have been alive and living in California. I know that this is quite a shock for you.

I must apologize for my deception. I have obtained a copy of my biography (along with all your other books) and was both pleased and flattered at your descriptions of my early work.

I know that you must have mixed emotions about the error of my death. For reasons I choose not to reveal, I had decided long ago to close the San Antonio chapter of my life. Though your book brought me great pleasure, I decided to keep the misconception of my death alive.

Let me also reveal that I am a great fan of your work. Though I have never had the pleasure of listening to your radio show, I have called in many times under the assumed name of Stewart. Please also excuse that deception.

I must thank you for protecting and caring for my drawings. I had always intended to return to San Antonio and retrieve them but never found the proper time. I thank you for guarding them as if they were your own. I only ask now that that they be donated to Trinity University.

I'm sure you are aware that you possess all but one set of drawings. For years I have had to keep one set with me. I have sworn to the Catholic Church that I would never reveal its secrets. But I cannot with a clear conscience take these secrets to my grave. I now pass them on to you. Much time has passed, and I am the last of a long list of co-conspirators. The secret is now yours to protect or to share. Use your own discretion. I trust your judgment.

Sincerely,

Randall Hugley

The letter was both everything he had hoped for and a giant mystery. It addressed all his questions but answered none of them. He dug through the box, tossed aside a pile of packing peanuts and found a tube. He did not need to open it to figure out its contents.

The tape sealing the top of the tube was yellow and cracked. He cut through the brittle pieces and opened the container. Gently he pulled out the large sheets of paper and unrolled them on the table. They quickly rolled back up again. He went over to the bookshelf and pulled four books from a shelf, causing the whole piece of furniture to collapse and its contents to spill to the floor. The door burst open, and the lawyer and David Whitehall rushed in.

"You okay?" the lawyer asked.

"I'm sorry, I've made a mess. Can you help me?" The three stacked the books back on the shelf with the help of a secretary. "I was trying to get a few books to hold down these blueprints," Taylor said as he replaced the last of the books. "That's what the package had in it, blueprints. Come look at this!"

A host of people gathered around the conference table, and again Taylor unrolled the drawings. This time with help, he used books to hold the two separate pieces of paper down. "These were in the package, along with a letter."

"What is it?" asked the lawyer.

"These are drawings to the St. Anthony Retreat, a catholic sanctuary just south of San Antonio."

"Are these the drawings that everybody seems to be after?" asked David Whitehall.

"Exactly," answered Taylor, as he closely examined the blueprints to the building. One page depicted the first floor, and the other page, the second story. The closer he looked at the drawings, the more frustrated he became.

"Why are these drawings so special?" asked the lawyer in a courtroom tone of voice.

"I wish I knew," said Taylor in a defeated tone. "Half of San Antonio is after these particular blueprints. A famous architect moves from the city he loves and lives the last half of his life in obscurity just to protect this set of drawings. And here I sit, the man chosen to possess them, and I can't figure out why they are so special."

The three of them continued to stare at the seemingly insignificant set of papers. "Two stories, two bathrooms, one small chapel, two sets of staircases, three small bedrooms, a kitchen and a study. What makes this house so special? Damn it!" cursed Taylor, as he took the original box and emptied its contents into a trash can, hoping to find another clue. "These drawings, can I take them back with me to San Antonio?" he asked the lawyer.

"Do with them whatever you feel is appropriate. They are yours now."

Taylor began rolling them up. "I have some associates who might be able to figure out why these are so special. Gentlemen, I thank you for your time. But I think it's best that I return to San Antonio with these."

"Taylor, if you have time before your flight, maybe you could come by our house?" asked David. "My wife just lost her father, and I believe that meeting you might help relieve her grief. That is, if you have enough time. I could give you a ride to the airport afterward," he offered.

Taylor finished rolling up the blueprints. "I would be pleased to meet your wife and the daughter of Randall Hugley."

* * *

Taylor and David walked into a modest but well-decorated suburban home. On top of the TV were a dozen pictures of what he assumed to be their children and grandchildren. "I bet you're hungry," David asked as he led Taylor into the kitchen. "We've been overrun with food. Why don't you help yourself?"

Taylor could not remember the last time he had eaten, but he knew it had not been that day. The kitchen was filled with fried chicken, ham, and a collection of casseroles and desserts. The news of the death of a father had obviously spread quickly and had brought a variety of covered dishes in sympathy.

He filled his plate with potato salad, a slab of ham, and a drumstick, not wanting to appear a glutton. He had a huge chunk of chicken in his mouth when David walked back into the kitchen along with his wife.

Upon seeing her, Taylor dropped the chicken leg on the plate and wiped his hands. As soon as his eyes hit Hugley's daughter, his heart raced. He could not believe who had just walked into the room. The face was so familiar.

"Taylor, I'd like you to meet my ... "

Without even waiting he engaged his mouth, wishing only seconds later that he had thought about what he had said. "I know your mother!"

The woman gasped and looked shocked. "You know my mother? What are you talking about?"

Both Taylor and the woman just stared at each other. David, sensing a disaster, jumped in to try to save face for both in the awkward moment. "Taylor, this is my wife Molly. Molly, this is Taylor Nichols, the young man who wrote your father's biography."

Taylor continued to stare at the woman in disbelief. There was no doubt in his mind that this was the daughter of Mrs. Floraman. Suddenly, many things began to make sense. Mrs. Floraman's inexplicable loss of composure when she told him that Randall Hugley was alive. Her futile insistence that he 'let things be'. The letter from Hugley stating that he 'decided long ago to close the San Antonio chapter of his life'. It all made sense now. "I'm sorry, but I know your mother. I mean I've met your mother, Mrs. Floraman, Edna Floraman, your mother," Taylor realized he was babbling.

"I'm sorry, but you must be mistaken," Molly replied, close to tears. "I never knew my mother. She died during childbirth."

Of course she did, Taylor thought to himself. Hugley had written that he had decided to close the San Antonio chapter of his life. He realized that he had opened his mouth way too soon. Here was a woman grieving over the death of her father, and he had just burst into her home and gleefully told her that the story that her father told her was nothing but a lie.

David took the hand of his wife and put his hand around her. "Molly, Taylor is the man who wrote the biography of your father. There is much he knows about his early life in San Antonio. I brought him here because I thought he might be able to tell you things about him that you always wanted to know."

The shaken woman walked into the living room, sat down on the couch and stared at the floor. "My father was very quiet about the early years of his life. It wasn't until today that I knew he was such an accomplished architect. There are many things I've always wanted to know about him. Perhaps you can tell me about him ... and my mother."

* * *

Taylor sat alone at a deserted gate at the Los Angeles airport. He appreciated the solitude after spending the day at the hospital, the law office, and at the Whitehalls'. Actually, his afternoon at their house proved to be very enlightening. Molly and David were enthralled with stories about Randall Hugley's early life in San Antonio. They fed him, laughed with him, cried, and hugged each other. As a collector of tales and lives, a historian, it was his most favorite day. The Whitehalls were so taken with Taylor that they offered him their guest room and asked him to stay for the funeral.

He would have loved nothing better. Unfortunately, obligations had to be met in San Antonio. He had come to Los Angeles looking for answers and left with the much-prized set of drawings and still more questions.

His plane was set to leave from an adjacent gate in a half hour, so he took the opportunity to stretch out in a vacant area. Earlier he had grabbed some free paperbacks from a Hare Krishna. Now he used them to hold down the blueprints, which he had unrolled on the terminal's carpeted floor. Again, he studied the drawings, hoping that something magical would pop up, something that would reveal itself to him.

Passersby paid little attention to the obsessed writer studying the valued prints. The only person who seemed to care was a 12-year-old boy who wandered over, bored with the tedious pace of air travel. "Whatchya looking at, Mister?"

"Just some blueprints of an old house."

"Is this your house?" the kid pestered.

"No," Taylor replied in a tone that subtly indicated that he wanted to be left alone.

"Is this a special house or something?"

"Yes, it's a mystery house," he said sarcastically. "You have to look at this blueprint and find out what makes this house different from all the others." He kept his head down and ignored the kid, hoping that he would go away.

"Where's the third page?"

"What?" he said, annoyed.

"Where's the third page, the one with the basement on it?" the kid said looking over Taylor's shoulder.

"What makes you think this house has a basement?"

"Because," said the kid, "you've got a set of stairs going down into the basement, but you've got no basement." The kid pointed to the drawing. Taylor looked and saw exactly what the kid had realized instantly. There were two sets of staircases, but one led between the first and second story and the other obviously led to a basement. He should have noticed it sooner. The blueprints for the second story only had one set of stairs leading up to them. That second set of stairs leaving the kitchen had to be going down. Down to a basement.

That was it. The building had a basement. And in that basement was something that both Noel Black and Father Olivares and the diocese wanted to make sure remained hidden. Suddenly, a lot of things were clear to him.

Both Black and Olivares had assumed that he had in his possession the blueprints to the retreat. And, for some reason, they wanted to make sure that the items stored in the basement would not become known to the general public. That is why a man like himself was so dangerous to the both of them.

What could it be? There was only one way to find out. He was going to have to go there and find out for himself.

He looked up to thank the kid for unlocking the mystery, but he had already wandered off to pester someone else.

Chapter 23

Joe waited patiently for a half hour at the San Antonio airport. It had been a long night already. Both of the Guenther brothers, along with Eric Bob and Steve, had spent most of the evening compiling the information they had gathered at the courthouse over the past few days. The work had been staggering but worth the effort. The Travis Club could finally get a handle on what they were dealing with.

"Know what you are up against," his father had always told him. José Reyes, Sr. had always believed in the power of the little man. "One man can fight the system; one man can make a change." He not only believed it, he lived it. As a boy he lived in poverty on San Antonio's West Side, working as a pecan sheller. Later, he was hired on as a civil servant at Kelly Air Force Base and was able to buy a house outside the barrio, send his kids to Catholic school, and otherwise enjoy the trappings of middle class life. But it was not enough for him.

He saw that others like him were satisfied with their gains in life. After all, their ascension had been dramatic. Many literally went from going to church barefoot to arriving in a Buick. But, José Reyes saw a different reality. He looked at the city fathers and saw few faces that looked like his. He looked around his neighborhood, and saw dirt roads and drainage ditches that overflowed with water from the North Side every time it rained. He saw public school students in dilapidated buildings, with un-air-conditioned classrooms on 100-degree days, while students on the other side of town learned in a safe and clean environment.

But what really bothered José Sr. was the inability to participate in the city's decision making process. Those who guided the destiny of the city made sure that people like José Reyes, Sr. had no say. The city council was pre-chosen by the business community and elected at large. The districts were non-existent, insuring that citizens like himself would never be able to serve. San Antonio was 55 percent Hispanic, but its city council was lily-white.

Instead of accepting the status quo, José Reyes decided to change it, in the only way he knew how. He organized the neighborhood churches, staged sit-ins, and disrupted city council meetings. The fire that burned inside him spread to others until their numbers were so large that they could not be ignored. José Reyes, the original monkey wrencher, had defeated the machine.

Today, however, another generation ruled San Antonio. This one had largely forgotten the efforts of José Reyes and had taken for granted his accomplishments. Children now grew up in a city that had Hispanic newscasters, councilmen, judges, doctors, and even mayors. The lines between Hispanics and whites had been blurred. But the son of José saw a different reality. He saw a city that had begun losing control to outsiders. And now the fire burned inside him.

That's what drew Joe to Taylor. Taylor had the fire also. He knew it the first time they met outside the soon-to-be-demolished Texas Theater. He knew that

Taylor would be the type to fly to Los Angeles on his last dollar. They were two of a kind.

Joe could tell when he got off the plane that Taylor had been through an emotional wringer. His eyes had dark circles around them, and his clothes were wrinkled. "Major, you look awful," he said sympathetically.

"It's been an unbelievable 24 hours."

"Are those the precious plans, the ones we have risked so much for?"

"These are them," Taylor answered, as they walked toward his car. "But they don't reveal much."

"Then what makes them so valuable?"

"Apparently, there is something in the old retreat that neither Black nor Olivares want us to see. And I have a feeling I know where it is hidden."

"What's our next step?" Joe asked, even though he already knew the answer.

"Well, I was wondering what you were doing tonight?"

"I was kind of planning on sleeping. It's kind of a new thing that's really catching on. You should try it some time."

"Sleep? There's plenty of time for sleep. We'll sleep in the morning."

"Excuse me, Mr. Unemployed. We don't all live the life of leisure," Joe joked, knowing deep down that he would not miss this for the world.

***

"Shhhhh, let's try not to wake Ella." Joe whispered as he unlocked the door and slipped into his living room.

"Too late, I'm already up," came a voice from the kitchen. "Did you bring the heretic with you?" Ella walked out of the kitchen in a robe and gave Taylor a hug. "I haven't seen you since your book signing party. You really are becoming the talk of the town. Father Parra mentioned your book in his sermon this Sunday."

"He's just bitter that his St. Celia's CYO basketball team sucks," said Joe, who always hated the fact that his wife dragged him to St. Celia's on Sundays.

"So, tell me. Did you really meet Mrs. Floraman's daughter?" Ella asked. Taylor realized that this was the kind of news that was going to spread quickly. He had called Joe from the Los Angeles airport and filled him in on the death of Randall Hugley and the package that he had left him. But, the news that he had met Mrs. Floraman's illegitimate child had caused quite a stir. The Guenthers, Steve and Eric Bob had all been at Joe's house at the time, and he could hear the buzz it created over the phone. Of all the information he had acquired over the past few days, this was the one tidbit that scared him most. He knew how badly this could hurt his landlady and he had not decided how he should handle the situation. He knew one thing: he loved her, and did not care to cause her pain.

"Ahhh, yes I did," he said, blowing off the question and hoping that Ella would note his discomfort with the subject.

"Joe, did you get the package?"

"No, Ella, I forgot." Joe quickly rummaged through a stack of items and found a parcel for Taylor. "Eric Bob brought this by today. It arrived at the radio station for you. Seems like Randall Hugley had one more item he wanted you to have."

Joe handed him the package and Taylor examined it closely. The return address informed him that it was from Hugley's alias, Stewart. "I checked the return address on the package; it's an address that doesn't exist," informed Joe.

"What could this be?" questioned Taylor, as he careful tore through the paper. Inside was a small handwritten note.

> "Taylor, I though this old book
> might help you with your research on
> your latest work concerning San Antonio
> and water. I love your show, Stewart."

Taylor pulled out a book from the package and quickly recognized it. "Ted and Ed gave me a copy of the very same book about a week ago," he said aloud. "I never got an opportunity to read it. It's an old book published by the city water department."

Joe, picking up the outer wrapping of the package, looked closely at the postmark. "We are some really great researchers. The postmark would have told us that this package was sent from Los Angeles."

"Well, that only makes sense now," Taylor replied, as he begun to thumb through the book.

"Read your book later, amigo; we've got some secret plans to investigate." Joe began to clear some space on the dining room table. It was filled with books, papers, photocopies of old records, and a dozen maps. As soon as sufficient space was cleared, he motioned for Taylor to hand him the drawings.

As he opened the tube and unrolled it, Taylor knocked a stack of books off a dining room chair. "Just put those anywhere," Joe stated in monotone, paying more attention to the precious drawings. "Okay, Major, show me what's so special about this blueprint."

Ella walked up behind them and handed Taylor a mug of coffee She looked over Joe's shoulder and peered at the map. He moved off to the side to give her a better view. "Obviously, this blueprint is very valuable to both Noel Black and to Father Olivares, Taylor began. "Why, I am not sure, but I think the answer is here." He pointed to the staircase, reaching over a stack of papers. "This is a staircase that leads down, but there is no set of drawings to the basement, my theory is that there is something in the basement that they don't want anybody to know about."

"So when can we leave?"

***

Joe and Taylor loaded two camping lanterns and a couple of flashlights into the back seat of Joe's car. Taylor climbed into the front with the blueprints and the book that Randall Hugley had sent him.

As soon as the car pulled out of the driveway, Taylor asked Joe to stop at a pay phone. "I need to make a call and I didn't want to do this in front of your wife"

Joe pulled the car into the parking lot of an icehouse and both got out.

He reached in his pocket for a piece of paper and a quarter and dialed a number.

"Hello, San Antonio Seminary."

"Yes, may I speak to Father Olivares?"

"I'm sorry, but the father has retired for the evening, perhaps you could call back during his office hours."

"Sorry, no can do. Wake him, it's important."

The man at the other end stammered. He was just a first year seminary student but already he knew he did not want to incur the wrath of Father Olivares. Waking him was out of the question.

"Listen, wake him up, and tell him he has an emergency phone call from Taylor Nichols. I'm sure he wants to hear from me."

"Hold on, sir." The student put down the phone. He had half a mind to pretend to have awakened the Father and to tell the caller to try again in the morning. But what if the call was really important? All he could think about was how he hated working the night desk.

"What's going on?" Joe asked.

"Poor kid, the last thing he wanted to do was wake the priest."

The two waited until Taylor could hear the phone rustle. He relished this confrontation.

"Taylor, thank you for calling," oozed the priest. "I was told it was an emergency. Is there some assistance I can offer?"

"I've got the plans. The plans for the retreat. I just located them."

"The plans! Wonderful, that's wonderful. I can't tell you what good news that is. Why don't you bring them by now? I'll wait up …"

"Sorry, but we're not coming within ten miles of the seminary. Not until you tell us why these drawing are so valuable to everybody."

"Taylor, come on in, and we will discuss it." The priest's voice began to shift from excitement to a cautious optimism.

"Come on in? We'll discuss it? For over a week now I've been followed. I've been deceived. I've been robbed. Now is not the time for a discussion. Now is the time for answers. Either you tell me why these plans are so valuable, or we'll just head on over to the retreat and find out for ourselves."

"Taylor, that's the last thing you want to do. Now be sensible!" The priest's voice began to get louder. Come over to the seminary and bring me those plans!"

"Sorry. Either you tell me why you want these so bad or I'm going to find out for myself. We are already on our way to the retreat."

"I forbid you to go there!" Olivares screamed. "I'll have you arrested for trespassing the minute you step on the grounds."

"Good try, but last time I checked, you no longer owned it. It's too late. We're outside the gate now." Joe looked at him and chuckled, knowing that they were a good twenty-five minutes away "Goodbye, father." Taylor hung up the phone and laughed.

"Did you really think he was going to tell you why he wanted those plans so badly?" Joe asked.

"No, if he could, he would have told me already. I just wanted to make his life miserable."

* * *

The car turned off the highway and on to a small County Road. "You know how to get there?" Taylor asked.

"Not really, I'm just looking at this map and hoping to find it," Joe said sheepishly, halfway hoping that Taylor would take over the wheel. But the passenger seat was right where the writer wanted to be. For the last 15 minutes his nose had been buried in a book that Randall Hugley had sent him.

"What are you reading?" asked Joe, desperate for conversation.

"It's a report of the city's water status from 1938."

"I can't believe this," Joe said. "Here we are on the verge of entering the St. Anthony Retreat, and you are doing research for your next book."

Taylor paid little attention the comment. "Did you know that in 1938, the city was already formulating plans for a reservoir? Ever hear of a place called Turkey Valley?"

"I'm going to drive this car off a cliff unless you put that book down."

"Great, whatever," Taylor replied, not allowing for a distraction. "You wouldn't believe how many questions this book answers. The whole thing is starting to make sense now."

Chapter 24

The car raced down a small country road on the outskirts of the county. "We're lost! Get your nose out of that book and tell me where I am."

Taylor put down the material he had been scanning. "I haven't been paying any attention. Where are we?"

"We're lost, that's where we are." Joe was obviously perturbed. "The retreat is supposed to be on this road, but I'm pretty sure I passed it." He looked ahead and saw a driveway he could use to turn around. "You'd think there would be a sign."

"Yeah, a sign. That's a good idea. And there probably is a smaller sign next to it telling everybody what's hidden out here. The sign was probably the first thing Black tore down when he bought the place."

"Hey, wiseass, you're welcome to drive anytime. You're the one who's been here before."

"Well, actually, I haven't been here before." Joe gave a disapproving glare. It was the single Randall Hugley property that Taylor had not visited. When writing his first book he carefully photographed every building, comparing the changes to the original design. Every building, that is, but the St. Anthony Retreat. Even then, the Catholic Church restricted access to the grounds. At the time, Taylor was told that the place was regarded as a sanctuary for meditation and that his visit would be too disruptive. But now he believed that had only been an excuse.

"How many different driveways and roads did you see between here and the turnaround?" Taylor asked.

"I don't know, must have been a dozen."

"We'll just have to backtrack. Stop at every one. Maybe we'll get lucky."

The first driveway they stopped at led to a small mobile home about 100 yards from the road. "That's probably not it," Joe joked.

The next two driveways were on the wrong side of the road. The fourth one looked like a definite possibility. They both got out of the car and looked around. With their headlights shining on the gate, they searched for anything to indicate that this could be the retreat. "Taylor, come check this out."

Both gathered at a rotting sign that had seen better days. Joe pulled back some weeds and read, "San Antonio Water Department, Turkey Valley Facility. No Trespassing. Weren't you just asking me where this was?"

"I had a feeling it was around here somewhere."

"You and your feelings."

"And I bet that the retreat is the next property we come to." Both returned to the car, shut the doors, and pulled back onto the country road. The next pull-off was a nondescript dirt road. "Stop the car for a second. I see something." Before they had even come to a halt, Taylor jumped out and began scurrying around in the weeds. He bent over, kicked around in a pile of leaves that appeared to have been recently piled there, and uncovered an old mailbox that had been uprooted. The side of the rusted box read, "St. Anthony Retreat."

"Bingo!"

He got back into the car, and they drove up the dusty road until their progress was stopped by a gate, chained and padlocked. The car rolled to a stop and

Taylor slumped down in his seat. "I guess I should have realized that this place would be locked up tighter than a drum."

Joe laughed and unlocked his door. "Well, Major, what do you suggest now?"

"I guess we should get the lanterns and flashlights and start hoofing it up to the main house. According to the drawings, it's a good two miles up to the retreat."

"Or, we can just cut the chain," Joe stated as he went to the back of the car and opened the trunk.

"Too bad we don't have a pair of bolt cutters."

Joe pulled something from the truck and walked around to Taylor's window. "Who says we don't?"

Taylor leaned forward with amazement. "Please tell me what made you think to bring a pair of bolt cutters."

"They're always in there. It's all part of being married to Ella. She told me that if I was going to chain myself to a toilet in a building that was about to be imploded that I needed to have a pair of bolt cutters. It was a little Christmas present. She won't let me leave the house without them.

"Are you just going to sit there or are you going to help me cut off this lock?" Taylor got out of the car and grabbed one handle of the bolt cutters. The thick metal chain was quite a challenge for the giant scissor-like instrument. "This is one of the many great things about Ella," Joe said, straining as he exerted his body weight onto the bolt cutters. "She's always looking out for us. Making sure we don't get caught chained to a toilet in a condemned building. I bet you didn't know that she waits up every night until I return home from our little missions. Sometimes she'll call her brother to go out and check on us."

Taylor grunted as he leaned into the handle. "Okay, Ella's a wonderful woman; I've always known that. So, what's your point?"

"I just don't want you to be soured on women because of your latest episode." The chain gave way with one giant push, splitting apart and falling against the fence with a clatter.

"You mean Logan? Well, I'm past all that."

Joe pulled the chain from around the posts and opened the gate. "Oh yeah, I forgot. The great Major Taylor, you are impervious to any type of heartbreak."

"The past week, I've been to Dallas, Los Angeles and back to San Antonio twice. I've had a book released, been accused of being a heretic by the local diocese, been fired from a job, stayed up two nights in a row to rewrite a book, found out my hero was still alive, found out he was dead again, and met Mrs. Floraman's illegitimate child. Believe me, thinking about Logan is the last thing I've been doing."

They walked back toward the car. "I know your life is crazy now, but in a week or so, there is going to be a Saturday night, and you're going to be alone at the library doing research." Joe slipped the key into the ignition and started the engine, "I know you, don't tell me that doesn't happen. You're going to be bitter and alone for weeks. You do this every time. Don't blame all women because another one screwed you over."

"You make it sound like I caught my girlfriend in bed with someone." Taylor pointed toward the road and motioned for Joe to drive. "She lied to me from the beginning, she was never even interested in me, and she was only there because she had to be there. I was just some project to her."

The car rolled slowly up the uneven dirt road. "Exactly my point. I'm just saying that you can't consider her having been a real girlfriend. Don't judge all women by her."

"I'm not. I acknowledge that Ella is as close to the perfect woman as you can find. Okay, can you just drive already?"

"I'm just saying ... "

"Drive!" Taylor turned, leaned over the seat and began collecting the flashlights and lanterns from the back. Joe hit a hole in the road, causing Taylor to slam his head into the roof.

"God, this road is awful," Joe said, trying to make amends.

"Kind of makes you wonder how often this place was used. With a road in such bad shape, you'd think that this retreat didn't get visited much."

Slowly, the car made it down into a ravine, and Joe parked next to a two-story building surrounded by scrub oak trees. "This is it?" Joe asked.

Taylor recognized the shape of the house from the blueprints, but even he was amazed at the size. The building was smaller than his apartment.

Joe got out of the car and walked to the porch. "I kind of imagined it a little different. I know this is just supposed to be a retreat, but I thought it was going to be some grand lodge located on dramatic hillside. This is just a little ... "

"A cabin in a ravine," Taylor stated, finishing Joe's thought.

"I thought that Black was going to develop this into some type of conference center?"

"That's right; this was supposed to be some elaborate corporate retreat or something. Seeing this now makes you wonder why this place is so coveted."

Taylor grabbed a rock, walked up on the porch, and looked inside a window. "I say we go in." The author took a step back and hurled the rock through the front window, which shattered into pieces. He then took a chair from the porch and began to knock the remaining pieces of glass from the frame.

Joe watched for a moment, then turned the handle to the front door and pushed it open. "Hey, it's unlocked."

Blushing, Taylor put down the chair and walked through the open door. "Don't worry, Major, you looked really cool knocking out that window."

Joe tried in vain to flip on the light switch. "Joe, do you really think there is going to be electricity?" Taylor asked, amused.

"No, but I didn't think the front door was going to be unlocked either." Joe returned to the car, turned off the headlights, grabbed a flashlight and tossed another one to Taylor. He took lanterns for both of them and stuck the tube with the blueprints in the back of his pants. With the lanterns fired up, they re-entered the retreat. The house was empty of furniture. Clean squares on the walls revealed where paintings had once hung. Bare light fixtures hung with their bulbs missing. "It looks like someone cleaned this place out," Joe observed, as he walked into the barren, dusty kitchen. A broom and worn-out mop leaned up against the sink.

"I'm surprised to find it empty. Father Olivares told me he wanted to get the blueprints so that he could retrieve some religious artifacts that were left in the house."

"Looks as if the good father lied."

The pair continued to wander, with Joe walking upstairs, only to find more abandonment. "Nothing up here but a great view of the giant ditch this place sits in."

"Notice anything missing in here?" Taylor questioned.

"Besides the furniture, the things on the wall, the fixtures and the electricity? No, it seems like everything else is here."

Taylor walked into the dining room, "Your observation is duly noted. But, where is the stairwell that leads to the basement?"

Joe removed the tube from the back of his pants. "Good point," he said, as he unrolled the plans. "According to this, the stairs should be between this dining room and the kitchen ... about right there." He looked up from the blueprints and saw that he was pointing to a door.

With lantern in hand, Taylor opened the door, only to find an empty closet. "This obviously isn't it."

Joe looked back at the plan and then at the closet. "Don't be so sure." He crouched to his knees and crawled into the closet. Knocking on the floor and feeling the edges of the floorboard, he closely inspected the wooden flooring. "Grab me that broom from the kitchen." Continuing to feel around, he grasped the broom handle with his free arm and stuck it into a hole. Applying pressure to the handle caused the entire floor panel to rise up. "Ah-ha. I knew it was there." Together, they lifted the panel, turned it on its side and carried it out of the closet, uncovering a stairwell. "Taylor, if you have ever read anything about Randall Hugley, you know the architect was known for designing hidden compartments, staircases ... "

"Really funny," smirked Taylor, when he realized Joe was quoting from one of his books.

Both looked into the stairwell and shined the lanterns into the dark hole. "After you, Major. I know you can't wait to go down into that hole."

Taking the first step into the dark narrow stairwell, Taylor tested the wooden plank staircase. Each step was deliberate and careful. Joe followed right behind, uncomfortably noticing the creaks that occurred with each movement. At the bottom of the stairs their halos of lantern light revealed a hallway with cut stone walls. Taylor walked quickly and followed the walls around a corner. Looking back, he noticed nothing but blackness behind him. Seconds later, he saw Joe turn the corner. "Did your lantern go off back there?"

"No, it's like a cave in here. I couldn't see yours either when you turned the corner. Don't go so fast." The duo continued to ramble through the underground passageway, stopping only to notice a change in the wall.

"Check this out! It's like we've entered some kind of cave or something. The cut stone wall just ends here," Taylor noted.

"How long have we been walking down here? I don't think we're under the house anymore."

"I think you're right. It's like they built a cave under here."

"Or maybe," Joe added, "this cave was already here, and this house was built to hide it."

Taylor looked and pointed at him. Joe's point made a lot of sense. The longer they walked, the more apparent it was that they were no longer below the house but had entered some natural dry cavern. The walls were irregular and the floor ceased to be smooth. Sometimes, they had to duck to continue on. The further they traveled, the harder it was to get around.

Finally, the passage opened up. A cavern appeared. Taylor was the first to see it, but Joe could already tell by the way the light bounced off Taylor's lantern that something was ahead. The musty smell of death filled his lungs. The writer stood and stared at a room with glass cases, each glass case containing a rotted corpse. Shelves of skeletons, many still with hair and soiled clothes, lined every side of the cavern. Joe stood wide-eyed and gasped as he entered, quickly estimating that there were over 150 bodies. Minutes passed before either Joe or Taylor moved or spoke, often looking at each other in amazement and horror.

Finally, Taylor could stand it no more. He moved toward the first stack of cases and touched the thick old glass.

He reached out, ran his hand along one of the more ornate wooden frames, and noticed a small brass plate on the bottom. He rubbed briskly at the plate, removing years of dirt. He stopped and read the name he had revealed.

"Oh my God! I can't believe this."

Joe rushed to his side, looked at the nameplate, and gasped. He shook his head and read the name aloud. "Davy Crockett."

Chapter 25

"Here's James Bowie!" Joe shouted, as he cleared another brass plate of grime. A mad rush had begun to uncover and identify the corpses.

"Hello, Mr. William Barrett Travis!" Taylor squealed, as it became more and more apparent what they had discovered.

"Last one to find James Bonham buys the tacos," Joe challenged. He knew that eventually the remains of James Bonham would be found, as would the other defenders of the Alamo.

Few historians ever are lucky enough to make a discovery that will forever change the past, or at least how people view it. Most that write and study the past realize that history is often not based on fact but on one-sided accounts recorded in journals, newspapers, or letters. And perhaps no historic tale is formed with as many half-truths and legends as the Battle of the Alamo.

After all, there were no surviving defenders to recount the events of the battle. Taylor knew what this newly uncovered catacomb would mean to historians, to the state, and the city. This would be the biggest news since the battle itself.

"Do you know what we are sitting on?" Joe laughed. "The biggest damn news story of the year. We're in the Alamo catacombs. The real burial place of Davy Crockett!" He picked up his lantern and looked across the tomb. "So ... what do we do now?"

"Let's go get a video recorder, a camera, something ... take some pictures. Get ready to show the world what's down here." They picked up their lanterns and trekked back through the narrow cave toward the stairs.

"I still don't get this," Joe said. "What does all this have to do with the North Side, with you? Why is this such a big secret? I thought this was supposed to be the answer to every question. I'm just more confused than ever."

Their pace was filled with excitement. They raced through the cave, past the stone hallway, and up the stairs. Back in the dining room of the old house, they paused to catch their breath. "Joe, this answers every question. This all makes perfect sense. There had to be something in that basement that both Black and the church wanted to remain a secret. I could have never guessed what it was, but now it all makes perfect sense."

"None of this makes any sense." Joe contradicted. "Why would the Catholic Church hide something like this for over a century?"

"Think back to after the battle. What happened to the Alamo? The Catholic Church tried to reclaim it. But the U.S. Government said it was theirs. Later, the state took over control. A mission built by the Catholic Church, now the state's largest tourist attraction, and the church has lost total control of it. My guess is that the bodies were brought here to this natural cavern after the battle. Later, when the church realized that they would lose control of the Alamo, they decided to keep quiet about the catacombs. After all, the church has a special place for those who died defending the mission, even if it was an abandoned one. They probably didn't want to risk losing control of the defenders' final resting place."

"Ok, I'll give you that," said Joe, once again assuming a courtroom tone. "But, why did the church sell this to Black? And why did he want it so bad? And what does this have ... "

"One question at a time, my friend. I learned something tonight that I never knew. Something that helped put everything together. Remember the book that Randall Hugely sent me?"

"The old water department book."

"Exactly. Remember how I told you that the city was considering a reservoir project way back then?"

"Vaguely, I was trying to drive."

"According to that report, the city had planned to build a reservoir in an area called Turkey Valley."

"Which is right next to this property."

"Wrong, it surrounds this property. This piece of land sits right in the middle of one of the lowest points in Bexar County. Not only that, but this spot also provides the closest access to the water in the aquifer."

"So what you're saying is that if you were going to build a reservoir, this would be the easiest and cheapest place to build it."

"Once again, Joe, you have crystallized my thoughts," Taylor's excitement brought a smile to Joe's face. "That's what the city thought when it decided to build the project over 50 years ago. Only there was one roadblock."

"These catacombs. So, the whole project gets canceled. But, let me guess." Joe leaned up against the wall as if it were a jury box. "Rumors of the Alamo catacombs start to spread around the city. So, to put a lid on them, the church puts together a little dog and pony show and 'accidentally' discovers a letter from Juan Seguin that says there are remains under the altar at the cathedral. Miraculously, remains are unearthed during a renovation project and sealed in a tomb in the front of the building for every tourist in the world to see. The rumors die down and everybody is happy."

Taylor added to his thoughts, "and they hire a noted architect to build this retreat over the cave entrance so no one ever happens to stumble across the real remains.

Nobody suspects anything until I happen to write a book disclaiming the validity of Davy Crockett's tomb 50 years later."

"The Major! Wreaking havoc on an ancient mystery!" Joe leaned over and gave Taylor the high-five. "Okay, that brings us up to the present, but what about Olivares? Why did he sell this property to Black?"

"He needed money. Here he is, an ambitious priest in the diocese, right hand man to an aging bishop. He wants to seal his fate in the church, and he can do that by arranging a papal visit to San Antonio. But bringing the pope to San Antonio costs money. And according to Father Patrick, the diocese is desperate for cash. So, Olivares starts selling off pieces of property that the church rarely uses, including this little retreat."

"And there is Noel Black ready to snatch this up in a second, to build a conference center."

"Conference center? That was the last thing he wanted to build. Don't you get it? He wanted to build a reservoir. If the city had that, he could develop as much land as he wanted to on the north side of town. Buy the land now, at fire sale prices, and make a killing later when that land becomes open for development. It all fits, it makes ... "

Taylor's thoughts were interrupted by the sound of footsteps coming from the dark regions of the front room. "Very clever, Mr. Nichols. Very clever indeed." Their lantern light illuminated the face of Noel Black as he rounded the corner into the dining room of the old retreat. "You do not disappoint me. I anticipated your powers of deduction. Fortunately, I have taken this into consideration." From his pocket he pulled a nickel-plated pistol, removed the safety, and pointed it at Taylor.

"How long have you been there?" Joe asked.

"Long enough to realize that you now know too much. I got a call from Olivares that you were headed here."

"Then we were right, you are planning to build a reservoir?" Taylor asked, as his hands moved into the air hoping to prolong the inevitable.

"For the most part. I don't just plan to build a reservoir. I plan to own the reservoir. And it's all legal. As you know, the state allows property owners to pump as much water as they please from under their land. I'll have the power to literally suck dry the aquifer, if I choose. I can bring the city to its knees. They'll have no choice but to rezone the land on the North Side at my request. I stand to make billions, literally billions.

"So, you see, Mr. Nichols, I cannot afford to have you ruin my plans. I tried to be nice about it. I tried to get you a safe corporate job where I could keep an eye on you. But you turned down Ms. Pierce's offer. What a foolish choice."

"I don't understand. Why did you feel you had to get rid of me?"

"As you once said, 'No one is more dangerous than a man who has nothing to lose.' I just could not have you and your motley band of monkey wrenchers messing around. There was just too much money at stake. And your timing was unfortunate. First, a book about Davy Crockett's tomb. I tried desperately to get an advance copy. I bought your book the day it was released just to see what you already knew.

"And then, another book planned about San Antonio's water supply. You were just poking your nose in the wrong places. And that damned radio show. What problems you caused. I was hoping to do this an easier way."

"Was it you or Olivares who broke into my apartment?" asked Taylor, trying desperately to hide his fear.

"Olivares? Olivares is a panicky fool. He didn't know what was here when he sold this to me. The bishop told him about the catacomb and to get the property back or else. Then, like a child, he comes crawling back to me asking to repurchase the retreat. When that wasn't an option, they decided to make sure that the secret would remain buried forever. That is why they were so desperate to get the plans. They were scared to death that you would expose the truth.

"But it was I who had everything stolen from your apartment. I needed to know just how much you knew.

Not much at the time, but I knew you were getting close when you visited Dallas then started checking courthouse records.

"Too bad for you. A little knowledge can be a very dangerous thing."

"What do you plan to do with us now? You can't believe we are going to keep this secret," barked Joe.

"No, I'm sure I couldn't trust you with this knowledge. I'm afraid both of you gentlemen will have to die." Black's hand shook as he tried to steady the gun.

"You don't think you can get away with this?" Joe questioned, with his hands raised over his head also. "There are too many people who know we are here."

"Yes, but they will never know if you made it here. Soon, your bodies will be sealed along with Davy Crockett's. Sealed, never to be found. Your car will be taken to a chop shop and divided into a hundred spare parts. You will simply vanish from the face of the earth. No bodies, no grounds for murder charges. I'm sure there will be questions, but there won't be any evidence for answers. Works out rather well, wouldn't you say?"

"A little too well, my son," came a thick Irish voice from behind Black. Cold steel stuck into the developer's back. "Take your choice. You can either shoot one of the lads and die instantly or drop the gun and live."

Black stood there, choosing not to move a muscle. Joe and Taylor stared at each other in disbelief. "Mr. Black," came the brogue, "I ask once again for you to drop the gun." The man shoved the barrel forcefully into his back. One by one, Black peeled his fingers from his pistol until it fell to the floor. A foot reached out and shoved it away from the both of them. "Eric Bob, pick up the gun."

"Eric Bob?" Taylor and Joe whispered to each other. Both were still holding their arms up.

From the shadows, Eric Bob emerged, picked up the gun, and pointed directly at Black. "Put your hands behind your back!"

Black obeyed, and the man in the shadows grabbed a plastic fastener and stripped his hands together. With Black secured, Taylor and Joe's savior walked forward from the shadows and revealed himself.

"Father Patrick? How did you ... what ... ?" stammered Taylor.

"I called him," answered Eric Bob. "Ella got worried and called me. I didn't know where this place was. So, I called Father Patrick."

"Where did you get the gun?" Joe asked.

Both laughed. "Gun? What gun?" Father Patrick chortled, as he pulled up a candlestick that had been fashioned from an Alamo rifle. "Thank God I had one of these."

Eric Bob continued to hold the gun on Black, who was visibly upset at the deception. "Your efforts are much too late. You are a bunch of fools. Nothing can stop me now."

"Keep talking, Mr. Black, you're on candid camera," said another voice from the shadows, "and you are about to be part of the biggest news story of the year." With camera in tow, Russell Rhodes stepped into the light. "A major developer attempts murder, threatens to blackmail the city, plans to destroy one of the most historical discoveries of the past 100 years... By five o'clock tomorrow, every news station in the country will be running this story. Not to mention pictures of Davy Crockett's tomb. I may not have enough light to take good pictures, but I sure got some dammed good audio."

Joe and Taylor finally let their hands drop. Neither could believe the timing of their rescuers. "I told you Ella looks out for me," Joe said to Taylor.

"You think this is over, don't you?" shouted Black as he faced the wall. "Well, it's anything but over. The wheels of progress have already started. There are a hundred people like myself ready to develop this city into their own image. There is too much money at stake. And you and your little band of merry men will be overwhelmed by what's coming after me."

"Keep blabbering, Mr. Black. The more you talk, the closer I'll be to a Pulitzer Prize," smiled Russell, as he continued to roll the camera. Realizing that it was in his best interest to keep quiet, Black finally shut his mouth, hung his head and turned it from the lens.

"I'll take this guy outside. Then we can call the police," Eric Bob said proudly, as he pointed toward the door with Black's gun.

Taylor and Joe watched in astonishment as Black was led from the building. Russell moved the camera lens toward them and announced "Cut!" as if he were making a movie. Reaching into a backpack, the television reporter got a fresh tape and continued, "Why doesn't someone show me the tombs? I'd love to get these pictures out by morning."

Joe led Russell down the stairs and into the tunnel. "I knew you guys were going to lead me to a big story!" Russell's laughter echoed all the way down into the cave.

Alone in the room with one lantern left blazing were Father Patrick and Taylor. "Father, you knew all along what was in the basement, didn't you?"

"Yes, I knew," said the priest in his rich accent while putting his arm around Taylor.

"And there never was a man named Merced following me either, was there?" asked Taylor.

"At the beginning there was, but only for a short time."

"I figured that out when I read a story in the paper about a church investigation along the border. I figured this Merced couldn't be in two places at once," stated Taylor. "But, why the deception?"

"I knew why this place was special and that it should be saved. Bishop O'Malley allowed me to see it when I was his personal assistant.

"But, I realized that if I spoke up, the church would have just shipped me off to some remote parish in South Texas. I knew that you would be able to reveal the story in your own way.

"But time was short, it wouldn't be long before Black would have cemented the cave shut and the catacomb would be lost forever. So, I concocted the Merced story to get you to realize the urgency of the situation."

"I bet you can't wait to see it again."

"My son, I've doubt it has changed much over 50 years. A few more minutes aren't going to matter. Go ahead; I'll catch up to you after I regain my composure. It has been quite an evening for an old priest like myself. Just leave one of those flashlights."

Taylor took one of the remaining flashlights and disappeared into the darkness below to join Joe and Russell. The old priest sat down on the top stairs and rested his weary legs. From his top pocket he reached for a Travis Club cigar and lit it, enjoying the refreshing taste of the smoke as it filled his lungs.

Part III

Chapter 26

The hot days of summer gave way to a cooler October. When the rest of the country was experiencing the beautiful change of seasons, San Antonians were finally turning off their air conditioners, opening their windows, and enjoying the outdoors once again.

Taylor drove to the airport in his new truck. He too had decided to forgo the air conditioner and roll down the windows for the first time in weeks. He pulled up to the terminal to pick up his passenger. "Would you like to go to your hotel first or over to the house?"

"Let's go to the house first; I've waited too long for this."

The drive home was quiet, the silence welcome. The woman reached out and grabbed his hand. "I think you're more nervous than I am."

"I just want to make sure this is the right thing."

"It is," she answered, as they slowed to a stop in front of his home. "Don't worry."

Together, they walked up the front walk, he carrying her bag. "Let me do this?" he asked. Instead of continuing up the steps to the upper apartment, he knocked on the downstairs door.

They both waited in a nervous silence until they heard the knob turn, and the door opened. "Mrs. Floraman, allow me to introduce your daughter, Molly."

Tears streamed down the old woman's cheeks as she reached out and hugged her daughter. She stepped back and vainly tried to clear her eyes. Putting her hands on her daughter's cheeks caused Molly to cry also. Taylor put the bag down inside the door and quietly exited, heading upstairs.

* * *

Inside his own apartment, Taylor took off his shoes and plopped on the couch. Mr. Tibbs jumped on his chest and burrowed in for a nap.

Much had happened since the discovery of the Alamo catacomb. The nation was captivated by the historic findings, thanks mainly to reports by local reporter Russell Rhodes, who had a garnered a sweet job with a network due to his efforts. It was not long before San Antonio became the most talked-about city in the country, nabbing the cover spots of *Time* and *Newsweek* and dominating national news for the rest of the summer.

Sales of replica Davy Crockett hats skyrocketed as Alamo fever began to sweep the nation. Women even began to wear the fake coonskin cap as a fashion statement. Tourists jammed the already crowded mission.

But even before the Alamo-mania had become the latest fad, the tidal wave of discoveries had caused a ripple effect throughout the city. Arguments began immediately to determine who should be the guardian of such a historic site. The National Park Service had retained Joe as its lawyer to argue on behalf of its interests. The Catholic Church maintained that they should retain control of the site, an argument that held little water considering that they had legally sold the property. The man responsible for the sale had been moved from the diocese office into what was said to be a parallel position in a small parish along the Mexican border.

Even though Father Olivares had been relocated to a border town, his dream of the pontiff's visit looked like it might actually happen. The pope had been asked by the mayor to come and bless the final resting site of Alamo defenders, and the Vatican had shown particular interest in making San Antonio a stop on its next visit to North America. The bishop requested that Father Patrick spearhead the efforts.

One thing certain was that the reservoir Noel Black had hoped to build would never become reality. The city had taken steps to ensure that the land on the north side of the city would now fall under even tougher zoning restrictions to protect the aquifer. Eventually, the city would move northward, but at a time and a pace that would ensure a safe water supply.

As for the St. Anthony Retreat, the ownership was now up in the air. Technically, it belonged to Noel

Black. But he lay wasting away without bail in a federal prison on a host of charges, which included attempted murder and fraud. He would gladly sell the property to cover his ever-mounting legal costs, but it looked like the retreat would eventually end up in the hands of the federal government.

Even though Black's trial was expected to be an open-and-shut case, the event caused considerable media attention. Eric Bob Kaufman King had hoped to cover the trial in his new capacity as reporter for a local television station, but it looked like he might be called to testify. Already, his exposé on Black had caused quite a lot of talk around town, especially the piece on how Black had influenced a local radio station to fire a talk show host that the developer despised.

The radio station in question had offered Taylor his job back, but he declined. Instead he suggested that the Guenther brothers take over his old time slot.

Even Steve's life had changed dramatically since the discovery. The taco shop that had bought advertising on his taco car was bought out by a national restaurant corporation and they had commissioned him to build 50 such vehicles to help launch a new coast-to-coast fast food chain.

For Taylor though, the change was most dramatic. The national media spotlight shone on him the brightest. With the urging of his publisher, he postponed his book about water and wrote an account of the catacomb discovery. It took only a month to write and another month before it was published, released, and sitting atop the best-seller list. Negotiations were ongoing for the movie rights. For most writers this would have been the pinnacle of their career.

For the past few months, life had really been very hectic for him: his first national book tour, interviews, and being asked to testify at the upcoming Black trial. In between all of that he had managed to convince Mrs. Floraman to open her life and let her daughter enter. Thinking about that, he called downstairs to see when Molly wanted to be taken to her hotel. His call revealed that she had canceled her reservation and had planned to stay with Mrs. Floraman, which pleased him.

Getting off the couch, Taylor gathered some research that he had been working on and was stuffing the papers into a knapsack when someone knocked at the door.

"Come in," he yelled, as he continued to pack some more notes. Again, the person knocked. Taylor walked to the door without looking through the peephole. As soon as he opened it, he wished that he had not. In the hall was the last person he wanted to see.

"Hello, I hope I didn't catch you at a bad time," Logan said. He had not seen or heard from her since that night in Dallas, but she looked as beautiful as he had remembered.

"I was thinking of going out," he replied, realizing that he had not asked her in. He couldn't help but smell her perfume as it drifted into his apartment.

"I was in the neighborhood and I thought it might be a good idea if we talked. I read your book and I heard it was going to be made into a movie."

"And you just wanted to drop by and see how you were going to be depicted?"

"I guess I deserve that." She looked down at the floor. "May I come in?"

"I don't think that would be a good idea."

"Look, I don't know why I came by. I just feel really awful about the way I treated you. The way Noel described you, I thought you were going to be some egotistical, womanizing jerk. I know you won't believe this, but I really thought I was doing the right thing at the time. Now, in hindsight, I realize what was really going on and I feel just terrible about what I did to you. You didn't deserve to be lied to and deceived."

"If you are apologizing—"

"I'm not looking for your forgiveness. I don't want to fool myself into thinking that you'd really give it to me. I just wanted you to know that I think ... " She stood there and looked into his eyes, seeking sympathy. "I just wanted you to know ... that ... Major Taylor was the first African American world champion in the history of sports. Born in Indianapolis, he achieved fame in the world of cycling during the turn of the century when it was a major worldwide sport. He pioneered new training techniques and was a champion in the U.S., Australia, and Europe. At the height of his popularity, he was a household name, but history forgot him and he died in obscurity." She turned and ran from his door. Taylor just let her go.

* * *

Taylor threw his knapsack into his truck and headed out. The pack was filled with notes and documents for his new book on San Antonio's water supply, despite offers to work on a screenplay for his previous book. He knew that his place for now was here. Driving alone, he thought of something that Noel Black had once said to him. "One man's history is another man's burden." It made so much sense to him. Some willingly choose to accept that burden, while others turn their backs.

Heading into downtown, he took his time. He was in no rush. Even though he had plenty of work to do, it was Saturday night and he knew that he would have the library all to himself.

####

ABOUT THE AUTHOR

Radio listeners in Dallas/Fort Worth may know Mark Louis Rybczyk better as 'Hawkeye,' the long time morning host on heritage country station, 96.3 FM KSCS. Award-winning disc jockeys, Mark, along with his partner Terry Dorsey, have the longest-running morning show in Dallas.

Mark is an avid skier, windsurfer and traveler. He is also the host of 'Travel With Hawkeye' a radio and television adventure feature that airs across the country. Visit the Travel With Hawkeye website at: TravelWithHawkeye.com

The Travis Club is the third book from Mark Louis Rybczyk. His other books are:

> *San Antonio Uncovered* by Mark Rybczyk
>
> *The Single Man* by John Paschal and Mark Louis

Follow Mark Louis Rybczyk on Facebook and Twitter:

Facebook.com/HawkeyeOnAir

Twitter: @HawkeyeOnAir

Learn more about The Book and Mark:

TheTravisClub.com

Or write to Mark:

Mark@TheTravisClub.com

Made in the USA
San Bernardino, CA
15 November 2013